Queen of the City

The Life of a Female Rapper

An Urban Hood Romance

Tamicka Higgins

© 2015

Disclaimer

This is a work of fiction. Names, places, characters and events are all fictitious for the reader's pleasure. Any similarities to real people, places, events, living or dead are all coincidental.

This book contains sexually explicit content that is intended for ADULTS ONLY (+18).

Introduction

I could hear the crowd chanting from inside my dressing room. I was in there, alone. It was by choice, though. It was the only way I could get in my zone before a big show, and I've done it countless times, but every time before I went on stage, I was still nervous. The anxiety shot through my body like heroin and for a moment, everyone quieted down. My heart beat was loud enough to break my eardrums as I sat in my chair, knowing my moment was just seconds away.

Boom! Boom! Boom! He knocked, then opened the door and stuck his head in, "Suzie, you ready?"

I didn't say a word. I glanced at him and nodded my head, letting him know I was ready to go.

"Five minutes," he said, letting the door close behind him. I got up and followed him out. The crowd became louder with each step I took. Men and women stood around backstage with glassy-eyed looks and liquor on their breath. That was usually me, but not tonight. I owed this to Junie. I owed this to Big Mama. I owed this to everyone who believed in me when shit was fucked up. I had to give it my all.

The DJ hyped the crowd up, "Are y'all ready?"

The crowd yelled out, "Yeah!" in response.

"No, no, no, I can't fuckin' hear y'all. That shit ain't loud enough. I said, ARE Y'ALL READY!"

"Hell yeah!"

"Here is the one all y'all been waitin' for! Suziiiiiie Rock!"

I stepped on the stage; the crowd went crazy. Chicks were in the front row damn near flashing me their breasts. Thirsty ass niggas were crowding the stage, reaching their arms out towards me when I stepped on. I had my head down as the chants continued, "Suzie! Suzie! Suzie!" I put my hand up to silence them. The DJ stopped spinning the record and for a moment, one surreal moment, the whole auditorium was bone silent. I lifted my head up, looking slowly from left to right. I held the microphone to my mouth and started rapping as the crowd went into another frenzy. This was my life, and I enjoyed every bit of it.

For me, it all started when I was back in high school. I came to the lunch table that Junie was sitting at with the rest of his home boys. He leaned over to kiss me as he made a beat with his hands on the table. The niggas around him all took turns spittin' lines to the beat. I sat there eating a bag of chips, just listening to them spit their shit. All of a sudden, it came around to me. Every muthafucka at the table was looking at me expecting to spit something.

"Y'all, get the fuck outta here with that shit. Y'all know I ain't wit' it."

"Come on, Lyric! I mean, god-damn, yo' fuckin' name is Lyric! You can spit somethin'."

I looked at Junie as he smiled at me, the beat he made on the table was still going. I put my bag of chips down, and their eyes widened out of shock, still not believing I was about to spit something.

"Suzy bedrock the mic/flow dirty like flintstone toes/dope lines out my mouth niggas get high when they hear me like they blowin' dro/muthafuckas hear me rap, and they swear I ain't write my shit/so I commit suicide and tell them I'm the ghostwriter."

The looks on their faces were priceless. I picked up my bag of chips and started eating them again as Junie stopped making the beat and everyone at the table dropped their jaws.

"What?" I said, looking back at them as I crunched on my chips.

"Fuck! What the fuck?! Where you get that shit from!?"

I laughed, "I got it from my head, dumbass. See, this is exactly why I don't like rhyming and shit because you muthafuckas don't like to let bitches get credit for shit!"

"Calm down, Lyric," Anthony said, "We... or I, I don't know about these other niggas, but I didn't know you had that in you."

"I didn't know you had it in you either," Junie spoke up, "and you're supposed to be my fuckin' girl and shit."

From that point on, niggas didn't call me Lyric no more. They called me Suzie. Suzie Rock. That's what the streets knew me by, and that's what I accepted. Suzie Rock. Suzie Muthafuckin' Rock.

Chapter 1

He sat outside in his Black Tahoe in front of my house waiting for me to get ready. He had to be out there a good thirty minutes before I finally stepped out the house, but what the fuck did he expect? Shit. I had to make sure I looked my best. I never thought I was the one to have a boyfriend. Not saying I was into hoes or whatever, it's just that people told me I was too hard to have a nigga. Too much of a thug, but Junie didn't care. He said I was like his best friend. We did all kinds of shit together. Played video games, hooped, went to the club together. Let him tell it; I was the perfect girlfriend, and honestly, I didn't start dressing real feminine until he came around. I was known to wear sweats and fitted hats everywhere I went. It was just who I was, but Junie helped me see how beautiful I really was on the outside. My friend Shaunie was shocked as shit when I came to her, asking her to show me how to put on make-up and walk in heels when I was 17. The sex appeal actually helped my rap career so I used it more and more to my advantage even though, at heart, I was just a tomboy. Not when I was with Junie though. When I was with Junie, I felt like a woman.

I finally walked outside and got in the passenger's seat. A look of annoyance was plastered across his face as I snapped my seatbelt on.

"What?"

"What you mean, what? I have been sittin' out here for damn near an hour for your ass to come out."

"Junie, don't play with me. You already know how I do when I'm gettin' ready, I don't understand why you are actin' brand new and shit."

"Fuck. Yo' ass should just start gettin' ready a day ahead of time and shit."

"Nigga. Just shut up and drive before I walk my ass back in the house."

"Aight, aight," he grabbed my leg and leaned in for a kiss.

"Ok. Now that's better. Let's go. Fuckin' with you, we already late."

He looked at me, "Really Lyric?"

"It was just a joke, quit bein sensitive! Let's go!"

He pulled out the parking spot, and we were gone. Junie and I have been together since our junior year in High School. He asked me to go to prom that year, and five years later, here we are. He was a pretty successful producer, mostly doing local shit, but he was well known around here. And me? I was one of his artists. We formed a pretty decent team, doing shows locally and out of state every now and then. We had a lot of supporters but with that, there were always a few people that didn't like what we were doing for various reasons. Maybe we were getting too much shine or bitches just jealous because I'm with the nigga they want, or they're on some petty shit like that. It is what it is, though, shit; we were still going strong. I wasn't going anywhere, and neither was he. He glanced down at his phone while he was driving.

"Fuck!"

"What's wrong?"

He was silent for a minute.

"Yo, let me drop you back off at the crib for a minute."

"What?"

"Baby, please. I just gotta handle some business."

"The fuck, Junie? Yo' ass was just talkin' about bein late, and shit and you wanna turn around and go back?"

"Please, just let me do this."

"Fuck that, take me with you."

He glanced at me for a moment as if he was thinking about his next move.

"Aight, Lyric. Just… just fuckin' stay in the ride, though, aight?"

"Aight."

We drove about twenty minutes to the east side of town in a beat-up ass neighborhood right in the gutter. Going from hood to hood was nothing for us, but there was always an uneasy feeling when you're in a hood you don't know anything about.

"Yo, just sit here, aight."

"Junie, I'm not your fuckin' little kid. I'm good. Go handle yo' business and hurry up."

He shook his head and got out the truck, being sure to lock the door behind him. I watched him walk to a house across the street. Five dudes sat on the porch when he approached the house. I recognized one of them immediately. Big Tuck. He was a well-known drug dealer from the East Side, and he had his hand in about every drug deal that went on in the city. Two things he didn't fuck around with was his drugs and his money. I know of him, but I never met him personally. All five of them looked towards the truck I was sitting in for a few moments like they were unsure about it just sitting there. I pulled my strap out of my purse and cocked it back just in case. Eventually, they looked away from me, and three of them went in the house with Junie. I sat in the car with my finger on the trigger, checking all windows continuously. The sun was slowly dipping down just beyond the horizon as the street lights began to flicker on up and down the block. I nervously looked at the time on my phone; the minutes felt like hours. I saw a man walking up to the truck as I looked out the side rearview mirror. I cracked the window and pointed the pistol in his direction as he put his hands up.

"Hey, I wasn't lookin' for trouble," he said, peering inside the window. "Hold up. You Suzie Rock, ain't you?"

"Yeah, who the fuck are you?"

"My bad, G," he said, "I was just letting you know yo' boy will be out in a minute, you know what I'm sayin'? That's it. I wasn't lookin' for no trouble."

His gold tooth glimmered under the streetlight as he smiled in a way that showed he didn't believe I would pull the trigger. He must not have known what I was capable of. I rolled up the window as he walked away. Moments later, Junie nervously came out the house like he had just seen a ghost. I slid my pistol back into my purse as he got in the truck, wiping the sweat from his forehead.

"Whassup, Junie?"

He put the truck into drive and rolled down the street, not saying a word to me. I knew what it was about.

"Junie, why you still fuckin' with that shit, huh? Damn! Don't you make enough money from this producing shit?"

"Mind yo' business, Lyric," he said, not looking in my direction.

"Fuck that. You are bein' stupid as fuck right now."

"Lyric, for real. Just mind yo' fuckin' business. I told yo' ass not to come anyway. It's yo' fuckin' fault I almost—" He cut his words short as I sat and waited for him to continue.

"You almost what, Junie?"

He pressed his foot on the gas, increasing the speed of the truck. I faced forward and kept silent for the rest of the ride to the party. Junie wasn't himself for the remainder of that night. It was almost like he was spaced out, his mind drifting off to places that nobody knew about but him. We finally arrived at the party. One of our friends was having a going away party. She was headed to the army, and this was probably the last time she was going to get to turn up for a while. She lived on the Southside, about 20 minutes from where I lived. We all went to the same high school, and it was sad that she was leaving, but then again, I was just happy she was getting out of this gutter-ass city.

"Heeeeeeey girl," she said as I walked into the house, "'bout fuckin' time y'all got here. Hey, Junie."

He nodded his head and kept walking into the house.

"The fuck is wrong with him?"

I shook my head, "He on some bullshit, don't worry about that. What's up with you, though? You ready to leave the nest and shit?"

"Hell yeah, girl. Mama is fuckin' gettin' on my last damn nerve and shit, and I'm tired of workin' these dead end ass jobs, so fuck it. This the next best thing. Everybody can't be a fuckin' rap star like you and shit."

"Bitch, please. I ain't no fuckin' rap star."

"Not yet, you ain't, but that shit is comin'. Niggas ain't even flowin' like you out here. You got this shit on lock, trust me, bitch."

I laughed, "Word."

"Well, find you a blunt and fire that shit up. I know it's some floating around here somewhere. I'm 'bout to get back here, so these fools don't fuck up the kitchen."

Crash! Glass broke in the other room.

"You muthafuckas!" Adrienne yelled as she sped towards the back.

The party was packed with people we went to school with. People I haven't seen since we walked across the stage and others I see pretty much on a daily basis. Milwaukee is a small ass city. If you go to the club three weeks in a row, you damn near will see everybody in the town at least twice.

"Whassup with yo' boy?" Anthony said as he walked over and stood next to me.

"Shit, I don't know. All I know is he left Big Tuck spot and he ain't been himself since then."

"Big Tuck?"

"Hell yeah. That's what the fuck I said."

"Wait, you were with him when he went?"

"Hell yeah. In the passenger's seat."

"Damn. And you still fuckin' living? And he still fuckin' living?"

"Yeah. You see we are here, don't you?"

"Yeah," he said, shaking his head in surprise, "that nigga is ruthless, though. He doesn't trust shit, so I'm just surprised he let that shit slide."

Anthony took out a blunt and fired it up. He had taken a few hits before he passed it my way.

"Well, one nigga did try to creep up on me and shit. I got the .45 in my purse, though; you know what I'm sayin'? I had it aimed at him, and he walks up to the car like, 'yo', you Suzie Rock' and shit. I'm like, 'yeah', then he kinda just backs away and tells me Junie would be out in a minute."

"Word? Damn. So you probably only made it out cuz you a semi-celebrity and shit."

"Maybe. But I tell you this, though; I woulda took at least one of them muthafuckas with me had it went down. Word up."

He laughed, shaking my hand in agreement with what I said. One thing I knew growing up in this city was that you couldn't be seen as a punk because both niggas and bitches will try you anytime you show a sign of weakness. I kept a hard grill on me for so long that it just became my look. Niggas be thinking I'm mean and shit, but that's just the face I have. It's the face that I was taught to have out here. He gave me the blunt as I walked over to Junie with it. He was looking out the window, paranoid, when I walked up behind him. He flinched when I put my hand on his waist.

"Fuck! Don't be doin' that shit, Lyric!" he snapped back

I looked at him with an attitude, "The fuck wrong with you, nigga? Ever since we left Tuck's new spot you been actin' like this. The fuck that nigga do to you?"

He looked down at the blunt and took it out my hand, "Nothin' man, nothin'."

"Shit. Maybe that will calm yo' ass down a little bit."

We walked outside and sat on the porch while the music blasted from the inside. It was one of our tracks. I bobbed my head, spitting the lyrics out word for word as Junie inhaled the weed and blew it slowly back out into the night sky. I could tell he was beginning to relax. Whatever happened at Big Tuck's spot shook him up pretty good. I knew he used to fuck with him a while back, but after we had started making a little money off this rap shit, I figured he would walk away from it. I mean, shit, we all hustled for a time, here and there. Even me. Big Grandmama said I got that from my mother. She raised me after my Mama died from a drug overdose when I was 13.

She was a dope girl back in the day, but she ended up getting strung out on her own work. Big Ma said she named me Lyric because I was as beautiful as Tupac's lyrics in "Dear Mama." Big Ma could never say his name right when she told me the story.

"Yeah, she called you Lyric because of that rapper, uh, what's his name? Two-Shop-Occur? Two-Spot-The Curse? Whatever that ole, bald-headed boy name is, she named you after she heard one of his songs."

She even told me that Mama had some lyrics of her own. She was more of a poet, though, from what I read. Before she passed away, she had shoeboxes full of notebooks that she wrote all types of poems in. It was dope reading that. It was like watching my birth on notebook pages. Seeing it with my own eyes was so surreal. As far as my daddy goes, last I heard he was locked up in jail somewhere. I could only remember seeing him twice in my life. Once was when he left Mama's house early in the morning. The other time was the day they took him away to jail. I had to be about eight years old then. If it wasn't for Big Mama, who knows where I would've been right now—but here I am. Twenty-two years old and graduated from High School. Not too bad for a crack baby.

"Don't you hate when like… the Leprechauns and shit be talkin' and then all of a sudden they stop? Don't you hate that shit, Lyric?"

I laughed, knowing the weed finally got into his system.

"Here you go with these god-damned leprechauns again, Junie. Why is it every time we get blown, you start talkin' about these muthafuckin' leprechauns? I don't see them."

"Ssssssh!" he said, holding a finger over his mouth, "a whole gang of them muthafuckas is lookin' right at us. They muggin' us and shit. Hold on."

He stood up and put his hands in the air before shouting,

"The fuck is up, niggas? Y'all got beef? What? Come holla at me then. Y'all standin' over there cliqued up and shit like y'all 'bout to ride on us. Whassup?"

"Junie!" I said, jumping up to grab him. "Sit yo' ass down! Those are some fuckin' lawn ornaments!"

"Naw, them bitches is leprechauns. I know a fuckin' leprechaun when I see it!"

The party began to wind down around 2 am. People flooded out of the house either drunk or high, and the music faded lower and lower. We sat in the front room with Adrienne and Anthony, reminiscing about old times. Our high school years at Riverside were some of the best years of our lives. No bills or bullshit like that, just fucking around in class, getting blunted, and skating past with "C" averages just so we could say we graduated. Nobody expected us to amount to anything, shit, we didn't even expect it, but looking at our lives now, we got further than we thought we would. Adrienne was on her way to the Army, Anthony was in his second year of college at the University of Wisconsin-Parkside, and Junie and I collected a little fame rapping and producing. I mean, it wasn't picture perfect but shit, it was good enough for us. We gave Adrienne our last goodbyes and left her house.

The streets were pretty empty as Junie's high completely went away. The moon hung low and bright in the clear sky above us. A few crackheads wandered aimlessly down the street while we were stopped at a red light. One of them tried to clean our windshield, but Junie stepped on the gas, damn near knocking him over with his side mirror.

"Damn, Junie!"

"What? How that nigga gon' try to clean my fuckin' window at night with his fuckin' sleeve and no Windex. Niggas be trippin' out here."

He stopped at a gas station not too far from Adrienne's house.

"I'm hungry as shit, Lyric. You want somethin' out of here?"

"Grab me a soda."

"Aight."

He got out the car as a few guys were huddled around the door of the 24-hour corner store. I watched them carefully as Junie went in. When he came out, one of the guys got his attention. He reached into his pocket and made a seamless transaction. To the naked eye, he just shook his hand but to somebody who knew what the deal was, it was evident.

He got back in the car and gave me the soda, "Cherry, right?" he asked, smiling with a bag full of snacks. "You already know." He leaned in and kissed me on the lips, slowly. Sucking my top lip and then the bottom. I put my hand gently on his chest.

"Baby, you really 'bout to try to freak me in this parking lot with these bright ass lights shining the fuck down on us?"

He looked around, "You right. My bad."

He turned on one of our tracks and we headed down the main street. When we approached a red light, another truck pulled up on the side of us. The windows were tinted so we couldn't see inside, but the music was thumping inside of it. We couldn't hear the words but the bass vibrated the windows. Junie pulled out into the intersection, running the red light as he looked nervously back at the truck that stopped next to ours.

"You just gon' run the light, Junie?"

He looked back in the rearview as he answered me. "What? There weren't any cars coming anyway."

He drove cautiously, taking a right turn down a neighborhood block. It didn't take long for me to understand what he was doing. He reached into his glove compartment and pulled out his pistol, cocking a bullet into the chamber. He rode to the end of the block and turned back onto another main street. Two cars were already parked at the next intersection, waiting for the light to turn green. He pulled up behind them, looking through each mirror in his vehicle. I pulled my pistol out and leaned back in the seat. I saw him glance at the gun I held in my hand. He didn't say anything as he turned the music in the truck down low. The light turned green, but the cars in front of him didn't move. He blew his horn and suddenly, three men got out of the back seat and opened fire on our truck.

POW! POW! POW! POW!

"Shit!"

Junie yelled as he fired back and stepped on the gas, crashing into the car that was stopped in front of us. I ducked down in my seat further, firing shots out of the window as the truck plowed over the car that the men jumped out of. *POW! POW! POW!* More shots rang out as Junie turned the corner and drove full speed down the street, bouncing off parked cars like pinballs.

"Fuck! Fuck!"

"Are you hit!? Baby are you hit!?" I frantically asked as he kept driving.

He held his hand over his chest as blood poured around it like water from a broken faucet.

"Oh my God, Junie!" I yelled, placing my hand on his chest.

He started to lose consciousness as I tried to take over the wheel. We ran up over a curb before we climbed a sidewalk and smacked into a tree. The airbags released, knocking me backward in my seat. I felt a sharp pain on the right side of my body as we both sat in the car motionless. I reached my hand down to my side, and when I pulled it back my hand was covered in blood. Immediately after that, sharp pains shot through my side. I looked over at Junie. His head was on the headrest; his eyes were wide open. He hadn't blinked since I glanced at him.

"Ju...Ju...Junie," I said, trying my hardest to get the words out.

He didn't answer. I could hear police sirens and ambulances in the distance, becoming louder and louder. I called out his name again, but there was still no answer. Moments later, I leaned my head back and passed out.

Chapter 2

"How is the heart rate?"

"It's steady."

"Ok, great. Let's keep it that way."

She looked towards the patient, "You're going to be all right. We're going to get you through this."

She looked towards the other doctors, "How is it now?"

"It's stable."

"Wonderful, that's what I like to hear. Where is the scalpel? Thank you. Did the bullets go all the way through?"

"Yes"

"So, we're dealing with clean shots. That helps. Looks like the abdomen, left side, hip and chest were hit. Apply pressure there. How is her blood pressure?"

"60/40."

"She lost a lot of blood. We have to get that up. Hold on."

I tried to get up.

"Whoa, whoa, whoa, just lay down, sweetheart. Lay down. Everything is going to be all right,"

"I need some more morphine; it's going to wear off any second." She looked away to the other doctors.

Beep. Beep. Beeeeeeeeeep

"She's coding! I need Dr. Thompson in here right away!"

I felt myself fading away, my eyes shutting quickly.

"You're going to be fine, sweetheart. Come on, stay with us, ok? Stay with us!"

I drifted back out moments later, vaguely hearing the doctors speak around me. It felt like it was over. All the things I dreamed of being. All the things I wanted to have in life were suddenly crumbling right in front of me, and there was nothing I could do about it but accept it. I didn't want it to end like this.

***

I opened my eyes to an empty room. Tubes ran from my mouth and nose to some machines that were hooked up to my left. I took slow, deep breaths as a nurse walked up to my bed, checking the machines. She smiled as she looked at me and then she leaned in a little closer to whisper in my ear. I could only make out a few of the words, "... had his hand... you... you are still alive." I blinked, wanting to respond to her but not fully able to. I put her sentence together in my mind, though. I understood. God did have his hand on me, and I was blessed to still be alive. She walked away as I closed my eyes again, not fully understanding what was going on but knowing that soon, I would be better. I drifted off to sleep again.

Big Mama sat in the chair at the foot of my bed reading her bible. I knew it was her bible because there's no other book that thick that she could carry around. She heard rustling in the bed and turned her attention towards me. She was 59 years old, but she moved like she was in her early 40's. She always used to say it was the grace of God that kept her feeling younger than she really was. She took her reading glasses off as she stood next to my bed, stroking my hair, a tear caught in the corner of her eye.

"How you feelin', baby?"

The tubes were removed from my nose and mouth as I lifted myself up off the bed. Big Mama tried to stop me, but I pushed through it.

"No, baby. Don't try to get up, now. Just lay back."

"I'm ok, Big Mama."

"No, you're not. Now lay back down. You may be in a hospital bed, but I will still pull my belt out and tan your behind!"

I smiled. Big Mama was tough. She had to be raising me in Milwaukee. The youth around here didn't care how old or young you were; they would test you, but Big Mama seemed to earn the respect of the young teens around our neighborhood. Tough love is what she gave, and many of them didn't have that in their lives until they met her. She was like the mother hen of the hood. One of the last of her kind. I laid back down on the bed.

"Good."

She pulled the covers back over me.

"The doctors say you got shot four times. Twice in your hip, once in your chest, and one in your side. They say the one that hit your chest could have pierced your heart if it was just a few more inches to the left. God has his hand on you, baby. That's for sure."

"How long have I been in here?"

"Oh, about two days."

I slowly began to piece back that event that got me in here in the first place. The party. The leprechauns. I laughed to myself, *those damn leprechauns*, I thought as I smiled. My mind suddenly went to Junie as I tried to get up in my bed. Big Ma put her hand on my shoulder and said,

"Now, baby. I told you to relax. You need to lay down."

"Big Mama, where is Junie?"

She ignored me.

"Baby, we will talk about that later."

"Big Ma, please!" I tried to get up, but my strength wasn't back yet. Big Ma was able to keep me down. "Where is Junie!? I need to make sure he is ok!"

The machine next to me started beeping faster.

"Baby, calm down, ok?"

"Big Ma, just please, tell me where Junie is! Just tell me and I'll lay down!"

"Baby, baby," she said, then hesitated, fighting back tears. "Junie... Junie didn't make it."

I stopped fighting her and sat motionless on the bed. If it wasn't for the beeps on the machine next to me, the room would've been entirely silent. Tears rolled down Big Mama's face as she stood there, preparing herself for my reaction. Tears bubbled in my eyes like water balloons that were ready to explode.

"No, no! Noooooooooooo!"

I yelled at the top of my lungs, using whatever strength I had to flail my arms around. The machine beeped unapologetically as Big Ma tried to calm me down,

"It's going to be alright baby; it's going to be alright."

"Nooooo! They killed him! They killed him!"

Doctors rushed in immediately, moving Big Ma out the way.

"Her blood pressure is rising again; we need to sedate her. Hurry up."

My doctor looked towards me and said, "You have to calm down, please."

"They killed him! They killed him!"

I convulsed as the adrenaline began to push strength through me that I didn't have a few minutes ago. Three more doctors entered the room, pinning me down to my bed.

"They killed him! Let me go! They fuckin' killed Junie!"

They slid the needle into my arm as I slowly began to fade out. My fighting decreased more and more with each thought of Junie. His smile. His lame jokes. The first time we had sex. The last time he told me he loved me. Our chemistry. It was all fading out as I closed my eyes. I could still feel the tears falling down the sides of my face before I blacked out. It was over. Please God, take me too.

Two police officers stood in my room when I opened my eyes. They stood to the right, talking with Big Mama. I tried to close them quickly again, but Big Mama called me out before I could.

"She wakes. Baby, you alright?" she asked as she walked to my bed. I sighed, not knowing what to say to her.

One of the officers walked over to me and said, "I'm Detective Rollins; this is my partner John Williamson. We just have a few questions about what happened a few nights ago."

I sat up in my bed, still sore from the gunshot wounds.

"We are sorry for the loss of Tyrell Butler. We know that he was your boyfriend for quite some time, and we want to get the people that are responsible for his death."

Big Ma rushed to the other side of me, ready to hold me if I had another reaction similar to the first one.

"I'm ok, Big Ma."

Detective Rollins took out a pen and a notepad to begin writing as soon as I spoke.

"Look, it was dark that night. I couldn't really see anybody's face. I just know that three dudes got out the car and started buckin' at us. That's all I know."

"You don't know if Tyrell had any problems with anybody? I mean, this looks like it was premeditated."

I knew the answer to that. It had something to do with Big Tuck. One of the guys that jumped out the car was the same man that walked up to the side of the truck when I was waiting outside at Big Tuck's house earlier that day. Same dreads, same build. It was him.

"Not that I know of, officer. Junie was just a good dude, a producer, and he was good at what he did, you know? I mean, a lot of people hated him because he was getting a lot of attention but if you're expecting me to point them out, you'll have a shorter list by lettin' me tell you who didn't have a problem with him."

"Well, we know something was going on. He had drug paraphernalia on him as well as a glock. I mean, somebody who is not involved in some type of criminal activities wouldn't have those things on him."

I peered at them, "Oh, so y'all are going to victimize the victim? No, fuck that—"

"Lyric, watch your language," Big Ma said.

"Big Ma, can you tell these officers that I have nothing else to say to them. I need to get my rest."

I turned over on my side away from them and closed my eyes as another stream of tears began to fall. I heard Big Ma apologizing to them on my behalf as they handed her a card and asked to be contacted if anything changed. I wasn't contacting them. I already knew who was involved, and if Big Tuck found out I pointed them in his direction, I was liable to get me and Big Mama killed. He was just ruthless like that. A fucking killer. It wasn't time for that. Not even close to it.

***

His funeral was packed with people that we had both known since our freshman year at Riverside. People I hadn't seen in years, who had come back to Milwaukee just to pay their respects. His mother wanted me to sit in the front with the rest of his immediate family. They considered me their daughter and after five years of being with their son, they had been ready to call me *daughter-in-law*. He only had one other sibling, an older sister. She moved away to California when she was 20. This was the first time she had been back since she left. She put her arm around me as we sat in the front pew at Ebenezer church of God in Christ. It's the Church Junie went to the few times that I did know him to go. When it was time to view the body, I stood up and made my way around to the front. The doctors said it would be a few weeks with therapy before I would be able to walk without my cane. Just another reminder of the last night I spent with Junie. I refused help as I hobbled my way to the casket.

He lay there, with makeup caked on his face. He was still handsome, but it just wasn't the way I was used to seeing him. He had on a black suit with a white shirt and a black tie. *He looks smooth as fuck*, I thought to myself as I looked him over with a smile and a tear in my eye. Down by his hands was a small turntable that would fit on a keychain. They fit it right between his hands, folded across his chest. All around him were pictures of the things he loved. His parents, his siblings, a picture of us the night of our junior and senior prom. That damn Milwaukee bucks logo. I laughed because no matter how bad the Bucks were, he always defended them through thick and thin. That's how he was about everything. He was loyal to a fault.

I leaned my cane on his casket and bent over to kiss him on his cheek. The shell of who he was. I made my way back to my seat as the line of people wanting to see him grew.

Later on, I took the microphone.

"Wow. I mean… there is so much I can say about Junie. I've known this man for the past seven years of my life and… I always thought that we would be in this forever. I mean, we were, it was just that… forever was not as long as we thought it would be. My best friend in the whole world is gone. My man. My protector. My backbone. My producer. I mean, we were connected in every area of life, and now it's like…"

I looked over to the casket and fought back tears, "Now, it's just like… what next? You know? What is there for me to do next? I loved that man. I loved him with all my heart and God knows that. God knows it, but I guess he was needed somewhere else. I don't know why I pulled through, and he didn't."

Pow! Pow! Pow! Screeeeeech! My mind momentarily flashed back to the night we were both shot as tears finally broke through the levee that was holding them in my eyes. His mother rushed to my side, but I waved her back.

"I'm ok, Mom."

She held her place.

"All I know is I'm here, and he's not. But honestly, I feel like I'm not either. I feel like I'm alive but not how I was before, you know? Like a part of me is gone. And it is. My life will never be the same. I remember the first time we went out together, he was like, 'If I make the beat, and you be my Lyric, we will make the greatest song the world has ever heard.' "

I wiped a tear from my eye. "And that right there is the line he used to pull me in, and it worked because we were together the very next day."

People sitting in the church pews laughed for a few moments.

"Junie, I'm going to miss you and even though I know you'll always be with me, it won't be the same. I love you now, and I'll love you forever."

Chapter 3

I sat on the couch, flipping through channels as Big Ma came into the front room.

"Baby, how you feeling today?"

"I'm alright, Big Mama."

"You want anything to eat?"

"No, ma'am. I'm all right."

"Ok. Let me know if you need anything."

"I will."

I moved in with Big Mama when I got out of the hospital. Junie was at my place more than half the time when I lived there so I couldn't handle being alone. Big Mama welcomed me with open arms when I asked her if I could. It had been a few weeks since Junie died but I was still barely eating. I hadn't left the house since his funeral, but on the bright side, I was just beginning to walk on my own again. I fell a few times when I tried to walk without my cane. It made me feel like an old woman, but Big Mama threatened that if she ever saw me try to walk without it again, she would break my other leg, and it would take twice as long for me to walk. Although I knew she wouldn't, I listened to her out of respect. That's what usually happens when children are raised right. When they get to that age that they know they could hurt their parents if they wanted to, that respect factor kicks in.

A few days later, I was walking like I'd never been shot. I had gotten calls from a lot of promoters asking me if I wanted to come out and feature at some events they were doing but I turned them all down. I wasn't trying to get back out there. Matter of fact, I didn't even want to rap no more. When Junie died, all that seemed to go away. The passion. The fire to eat other Emcees alive on the microphone just faded. I didn't have my partner in crime with me, so it was all pointless.

I ran into my high school teacher at the funeral. After, she gave me her number and told me to contact her if I ever needed anything. She had a plug at a retail store in Mayfair, a mall on the city's north side. I tried it out. I had to. I couldn't just sit at the crib all day not doing shit. That didn't last long, though. On my first day, I got into it with some chick at the register because she said I wasn't ringing her clothes up right.

"Uh, excuse me? That is not $14.99. The ticket said it was on sale for $8.95."

I peered at her for a moment before I answered, "I'm sorry. I'll ring it up for the price you said it was."

"No, no. That shit should've been corrected before you rang it up in the first place. See, this the bullshit I'm talkin' about. Y'all never has y'all shit together up here."

I closed my eyes, breathing slowly, "It's ok. We just have to ring up—"

"No, bitch. Nuh-un, see, I don't like your attitude." She raised her voice, "Where the fuck is the manager at?! They need to teach their *employees* how to fuckin' talk to customers without rolling their eyes and shit. Where is the manager?"

I was never one to let anybody talk shit to me without doing anything about it. I took the clothes and threw them in her face.

"Bitch, you ring this shit up yourself."

She stood across the counter with her mouth hung open as I walked away. The manager came speed walking down the aisle as she saw me walking away from the counter. I took off my name tag and threw it on the floor in front of her.

"Y'all find somebody else to do this shit. I'm done dealing with…" I turned back in the customer's direction as she stood at the counter, yelling loud enough for her to hear me, "…dumb ass people like her!"

It wasn't until security crowded her that she tried to break through their grasp and get to me. I walked out of the store and never looked back. It was at that moment that I knew retail wasn't for me. I knew a regular 9 to 5 job wasn't for me. There was no way I could work a job like that when the only thing I've known was rapping and doing shows. I couldn't bring myself to that, though. Not anymore. It was about 3:45pm when my phone rang. LaQuandra was on the other end.

"Sup bitch, how you been?"

"Shit, I have been better."

"Word. Where have you been at, though? Muthafuckas said you been a fuckin' ghost since Junie passed."

"Hell yeah. I ain't been feelin' shit; you know what I'm saying? I have just been like… a fuckin' bum and shit laying around the crib watching cartoons."

"Big ass fuckin' kid."

"Hell yeah. It's what me and Jun—" I stopped myself, trying to keep the reminiscing short. "Anyways, whassup though?"

"Shit. Just tryin' to see if you wanna get out for once tonight."

"I'm broke as fuck, Quandra. I ain't got shit right now."

"Word. Hmmm…. Well, I might have a job for you, but you gotta come out with me tomorrow."

"I don't know, Quandra. I just… I don't know."

"Come on girl; you need to get out the crib before you get depressed and shit. Come on."

"I don't know."

"Girl, fuck the bullshit. I got you. You wanna go or not?"

"I can barely walk and shit, Quandra."

"Bitch, all I hear is excuses. You wanna go or not?"

I thought to myself for a moment before I shook my head and said, "Fuck it; I'll go. When are you leavin'?"

"I'ma go to the spot tomorrow. Just umm… wear something comfortable and shit."

"Aight."

Quandra was a gutter ass chick that came up with Junie and me. We didn't reconnect until Junie died. It was crazy how his death brought old relationships back together. She was good people, though; she was just hood as fuck, but I was used to it. She picked me up at around 11 pm the next night.

I took my time getting into her car. "You old as fuck right now, bitch."

"Fuck you," I said as I closed the door.

We had driven fifteen minutes before we came to the spot. I looked up at the sign, "Onyx? Really? A fuckin' strip club?"

"Bitch, just get out the car and come on. Damn."

We got out as she walked a few steps in front of me. She had on a short ass skirt that damn near showed the bottom of her ass cheeks. She tried to pull it down as she walked but it was useless, she was much too thick for that. She walked past two security guards as they let her through. She stopped just inside the door and waited for me. The guards smiled at me as I walked right past them like they didn't exist. She led me up to a dressing room.

"Quandra. What the fuck?"

"What?" She said as she began taking her clothes off in front of me.

"Don't act like you ain't never seen titties before, quit trippin'. Look, you were talkin' 'bout how you need a job and shit and you a fine ass bitch. I mean, I know you this thug ass rapper and shit and you probably ain't tryin' to have this look about you, but shit, if you tryin' to make money, these thirsty ass niggas got bread, and they will pay you for that ass. Trust me honey."

She slid on her thong and started tying up the strings on her high heels as she explained,

"I ain't worked a day in my life outside these walls, and you see all my bills are paid on time. Shit, if you play yo' cards right, you might even have some of these loser ass niggas in this club paying yo' bills while you keep yo' money in yo' pocket."

She laughed, "This is America. Shit. The American dream for hood ass bitches like me."

She walked over to the mirror as I stood against the wall. A few more thick women walked into the dressing room, eyeballing me as they walked past me. *I can't believe she got me in this fuckin' strip club*, I thought to myself. Quandra walked back over to me.

"So, this is what is about happen. You can walk yo' ass out there and sit in the audience. Watch what some of these chicks do to get paid. Then you tell me why you can't do that shit. Tell me why a woman, as thick and as fine as you are, can't go out there and shake that shit for some change? It's easy money. Easy fuckin' money. Now come on."

She led me outside the club and sat me down in a seat near the front next to the stage. She ordered a few drinks for me to loosen up. I wasn't uncomfortable. In fact, I'd seen women come on to me before; sexy ass women and it took everything in me not to give in to my curiosity.

"Suzie Rock?"

I heard someone call me out behind me. I didn't turn around. I kept looking forward as the man repeated my name again. That's what it was for me. I didn't want people recognizing me in here. I downed the three shots of Coke and Hennessey that the bartender brought over for me. I winced as it burned my throat and moments later, the music began playing, and LaQuandra came to the stage. She walked to the front as niggas yelled in the audience,

"Awwwww hell yeah, here comes my bitch! Shake that shit! Shake that shit!"

I leaned back in my seat, observing her. She spun around and slowly shook her ass from left to right, her cheeks following each movement a few moments late. She put the pole between her ass and shook up and down before she leaned forward on a handstand and wrapped her legs around the pole. Her ass was above her head as she still found a way to make her cheeks jiggle as she slid down the pole and tumbled into the splits, bouncing up and down on the ground.

"Hell yeah, work that shit! Work that shit!" a tall, dark-skinned man said as he walked up. He slapped a twenty dollar bill on her ass. She shook it harder as he pulled out another one and smacked it on her ass even harder. She spun around, opened her legs and shoved his face into her pussy. Another man ran up and rained dollar bills all over her. She looked over at me and winked as she let the man get up. She spun around again, facing her ass to the crowd and moved one cheek by itself, then the other simultaneously. Another thirsty ass nigga came and slapped twenty dollar bills on her ass. She got up and made her way over to the pole, spinning around on it as she loosened her top, letting her titties fall out. Before I knew it, there were hundreds of dollars on the ground in front of her as she gave these men exactly what they wanted.

Maybe I can do this, I thought to myself, *hell yeah, perhaps I can*.

Chapter 4

I sat outside on my porch with my feet propped up on the banister. The cool Milwaukee breeze blew onto my face while I rocked back and forth in my chair. Kids were running up and down the sidewalk and playing like we used to when we were younger. Before the PlayStations and the Xboxes came into the world and before the internet was readily accessible. It made me reminisce about my younger days when life was a lot simpler than it was now—when the less we knew about how the world worked, the happier we were. I unwrapped a honey bun just as an all-black Monte Carlo parked in front of the house. I knew who it was before he stepped out the car. He walked up the steps and onto the porch, making himself a seat right beside me.

"Whassup Tuck?"

"Shit. Just another day, you know?" He was somber.

"I hear you. When you supposed to go back to school?"

"Next week. Spring break ends quickly most times."

I repositioned myself on the porch and said, "I don't know shit about no spring break. I haven't been in a classroom since high school."

He smiled, "Yeah. I know."

A few moments of silence passed between us. A car drove down the block, screeching to a stop as a ball rolled out into the street. Seconds later, a little boy ran out after it and scooped it up. The car burned rubber as it sped off again.

"Muthafuckas drive through this neighborhood and shit like it's a busy street. One of these days these little niggas is gon' get ran the fuck over."

He didn't say anything. His eyes drifted off into the horizon like he was trying to make sense of something he didn't understand. Outside of me, he took Junie's death the hardest. They were best friends since 5th grade. What started off as a fist fight in elementary school turned into a rock solid friendship.

"I know you heard Big Tuck put a hit out on him."

I raised up from my seat, "A hit?"

He looked towards me with squinted eyes and said, "You really didn't know? Shit. That's all muthafuckas been talkin' 'bout round the way. Said it was some shit about him not havin' all the money he owed or some shit. I mean, I don't know the details of it all, but I'm just sayin' what I heard."

"A fuckin' hit?"

"Yeah. You know how that nigga Tuck gets down. Nigga got bodies on him and can't nobody do shit about it but stay out his way."

I felt the anger creeping through my blood. He was right, though. There wasn't a thing anybody could do about Big Tuck. The nigga had police officers on payroll and a lawyer that ate everything thrown his way. He was damn near untouchable but even with that, I felt there was something that could get to him.

"I hear you."

"Well, shit, I was just coming through to check on you and shit. I ain't heard from you since the funeral."

"Oh. Aight, yeah, thank you. I'll be aight, though, you know. I'm fightin' just like you."

"No doubt, sis. I'ma holla at you, though."

He got up and walked down the steps and back to his car, stopping another ball before it had the chance to roll out in the street. He tossed it back to the little boy who caught it and ran back to his group of friends. I sat back down in my chair as thoughts of Junie began flooding my mind.

Pow! Pow! Pow! Screeeeech! I kept seeing the truck speed off away from the car that was shooting at us. The sharp pain and burning sensation from the bullets piercing through my flesh. His face as his head laid against the headrest, his eyes wide open, blood spilling from his mouth.

"Lyric? Lyric?" Big Mama had to say my name a few times to grab my attention. "Come on inside here, baby; I got something for you to eat."

"Ok, Big Mama."

She walked into the house, and I trailed right behind her. Big Mama cooked dinner early. It was done by 6 pm at the latest, and she prepared the things that would stick to your ribs. Greens, Baked chicken, sweet potatoes, corn on the cob, and hot water cornbread.

"Dang Big Mama, you trying to get me fat."

She laughed. "Naw baby, I'm trying to keep you healthy. Don't act like I haven't noticed you ain't been eatin' good."

I sat down at the table. "I just haven't had an appetite lately."

"Honey, I know it's hard. Junie was a good man, and I know he was good for you, but you can't go about starving yourself. That's not gonna bring Junie back, and it's just going to cause you to get sick. Depressed. We can't let that happen."

"I know Big Mama."

"Good. Now, go ahead and eat your plate. I'm gonna' go in here and lay down but if you need me, just holla, and I'll be right here, ok?"

"Yes, ma'am."

She walked to her room as I glared down at my plate. Food just wasn't as appealing as it was to me before. Maybe Big Mama was right. Maybe I was slipping into some sort of depression because of Junie's death. I don't know. Maybe I just had to get out of town. A change of scenery could help me get my mind off of things, even if it was just for a short time.

My phone buzzed in my lap. It was a text message from LaQuandra: *So, what you think about last night?*

I replied: *It was aight, I guess.*

I talked to the owner about you. He said he wouldn't mind seeing you do yo' thang on stage with his nasty ass.

I don't know, Quandra.

Ok. Well, the offer is on the table if you feel up to it, but you gotta let me know because I'm going out of town in a couple days.

I paused for a moment before I sent a response back to her: *What are you going out of the city for?*

Business. I'm going to Chicago for a couple months to work at a club out there.

It seemed like the perfect opportunity for me to get away for a while: *What if I wanted to come with you?*

Shit, if you come, you better be ready to shake ya ass. Ain't no dead weight rollin' with me.

I put the phone down and forced some of Big Mama's food down my throat. Her food was always good, but the taste was just a bit off for me. It was more my mind than anything else, though. At that point, there was nothing else better for me to do.

I responded to her: *Ok. I'll work with you.*

I figured I would be more comfortable showing my ass in a city where hardly anybody knew me than at home. Here in Milwaukee, once you're recognized as a stripper, it's damn near impossible to be seen doing anything else. I didn't want that hanging over my head in my city. I forced some more of Big Mama's food down my throat, washing it down with the ice cold soda she sat on the table.

LaQuandra finally responded to my text: *Aight, cool. We leave on Friday then!*

Chapter 5

Big Mama tried to talk me out of going to Chicago with LaQuandra. She knew her since our freshman year in high school and to her, LaQuandra was nothing but trouble.

"That girl ain't got a lick of sense, baby. You sure you want to be going with her to another city?"

"I'm sure Big Mama."

I loaded my suitcase with clothing for the trip as I tried to explain, "I… I just need to get away from here. It's this city, and you're right, I was on the verge of being depressed here. It's hard for me to function without Junie. I mean, I got shot up and everything. I just want to get away for a while; that's it, Mama. Just a little while."

She paced the room back and forth. I couldn't tell if she just didn't want to be lonely or if she was really nervous about something happening to me while I was with Quandra. Either way, I knew she was uneasy with me going but I didn't have a choice. My anger towards Big Tuck grew every time Junie's murder flashed in my mind like a nightmare. The urge for revenge was increasing, and I knew that would lead to nothing but my death. The next best thing was just to leave. I stopped packing and turned towards Big Mama as she stood with her hands on her hips, watching my every move. The glimmer of tears sat right at the bottom of her eyes as I put my arms around her.

"Big Mama, I'ma be back, ok? I'll be back but… just trust me. I need to get away and clear my mind. That's it. I'm going to come back and be the Lyric I was before all this stuff happened. I just need this time."

She sighed, "I know baby, I know. You gotta do what you gotta do. I understand, I just… I know I almost lost you once, and I don't want to go through that again, hear?"

"Yes ma'am, I understand and you know I can take care of myself. You raised a tough woman. I mean, look at you? Don't you remember all the times you used to tell me how you fought dudes when you were my age because they were talkin' smack to you? All the situations you been in and fought your way out?"

"I remember. I remember, baby. But just because I got through it, don't mean I want you to have to experience the same things."

"I don't either, Big Mama, but just know that if I come to something, I'll be ok. I'll make it out. I always do, and you know that."

I put my hands on her cheeks and squeezed them together, causing her lips to pucker up. I kissed her on them, the same way she did when I was little. She laughed.

"Ok baby. I trust you. Just, hold tight one second, ok?"

"Ok."

She left the room as I continued packing. I slid a few thongs and some sexy lingerie that Junie bought for me into my suitcase. Big Mama was in my room the whole time I was packing so I couldn't put any of those things in there yet. It would have brought a whole line of questioning that I wasn't prepared to answer. She came back in the room with two books—a bible and a devotional for young women.

"Now, you take these, hear? Keep The Lord close to your heart. He is the only one that can protect you at all times."

Where was he when Junie died? I thought to myself as I took the books out of her hand. Big Mama's faith was unwavering.

No matter what happened, it was always in the Lord's hands to her. I would be lying if I didn't say that Junie's death brought some uneasiness with God in my life. Something that wasn't there before everything happened. How could he let somebody that I loved so much just die like that? In that way? I didn't understand it, but I tossed the books in my bag out of respect for her.

"Ok, Big Mama. Thank you."

I looked at the clock on my phone: 9:15 am. Quandra was going to be here any minute. She was driving to Chicago and wanted to beat traffic, so she wanted to leave as early as possible. She pulled up to our house right on schedule. She got out the car and walked to the porch just as I was stepping down with my luggage. Big Mama stood in the door as Quandra reached out to help me and greet Big Mama,

"Oh. Oh, hey Miss Sutton. How are you doing today?"

"Hello, LaQuandra. I'm well, how about yourself?" Big Mama peered back at her, a look that lacked any form of trust.

"I'm good, Ma'am. Thanks for asking."

She turned and walked back to her car with me. "What in the entire fuck is wrong with yo' grandma? What did I do to her?"

"She just remembers you from high school."

"Oh."

She paused, then turned it into laughter, "Well, I get it now. I was wild as fuck in high school, shit, no wonder. How about I just stay down here while you say yo' goodbyes to her?"

I loaded my things into the back seat.

"Good idea."

I walked back to the house as she stood there, worry dripping from her eyes like honey.

I shook my head. "Big Mama, I'm going to be fine."

"You call me when you get there and get settled, hear?"

"Yes, Ma'am."

"I'll be praying for you."

She reached her arms around me and held on tight like it was going to be the last time I saw her. I didn't like it, but I understood it. She said my mama left her the same way. She said she needed a break and next thing she knew, she was getting a phone call from the police talking about they need her to come make a positive ID because of her death. I understood her fear, but she didn't understand one thing—I was not my mother.

The car ride to Chicago went fast. We reminisced about old times all the way there, listening to old rap songs on her Pandora station and singing everything off key. I didn't have many female friends but for some reason, LaQuandra was the one that clicked back with me. The scenery from Milwaukee to Chicago was completely different. The traffic was heavier. Downtown had more life to it and overall, the city was just much bigger. More to get into. She drove to the club that we would be working at.

"Come on girl. I told him you were coming, and he wanted to meet you."

We got out of the car and walked into the building. It looked like it was vacant from the outside, but when we walked in it was an entirely different story. The carpet that led to the main floor was a plush, blue material. It felt like my feet were sinking into it with each step I took. There were mirrors on every wall in the hallway with bright vanity lights that lined the top of them. We headed to the back room to his office. Quandra knocked twice.

"Who the fuck is it?" The voice yelled from the other side.

Quandra shook her head as she collected herself, "It's LaQuandra."

I heard movement from inside the room before he finally unlocked the door and let us into the large office. He had mirrors all around on every wall, including the ceiling. Pictures of him with half-naked women were plastered just about everywhere in there. On his desk, on tables, hanging on walls. He smiled at me as we walked in. He wasn't much taller than me, but he was stocky. His hair was permed like an old-school pimp and a toothpick dangled out the corner of his mouth,

"Yes, yes Lawd," he said as we walked in. Quandra sat down in a chair in front of his desk as his wicked smile never left his face. He walked around to his side of the desk, licking his lips at us as I sat down next to Quandra.

"So this... this the girl you was tellin' me 'bout now, huh?"

She smiled at me. "Yup. This is her."

"Ok, ok. Well, stand up. Let me see that ass."

I looked at him with a side-eye. Quandra whispered to me, "Girl, just get up and let him see you."

I stood up and spun around. I saw myself in the mirror. I wore jeans that showed the round shape of my ass perfectly. My shirt was cut low, exposing the top of my titties.

"Yes, yes, yes, Lawd!"

He said as he clapped his hands at me. He walked from around his desk and stood right in front of me. I could feel his breath on my neck as he spoke.

"Damn girl, you fine as shit. Umm-hmmm, I think you're gonna do well up here. That's for damn sure. You are gonna do well. These thirsty ass niggas love a fat ass!"

He said as he smacked my cheeks. I quickly turned around as Quandra stood between us.

"Shit, and you feisty, too!?"

He looked towards Quandra, "Bitch, what took you so fuckin' long to bring her ass up here? That's all I wanna know. What in the fuck took you so long?"

"She just said she wanted to dance."

"Is that right?"

He licked his lips, "Well, dance you will. Dance you fuckin' will."

He walked back to his side of the desk. I didn't take my seat again until he sat down and began pulling papers from his drawer. He set them on the desk in front of him as he folded his hands and looked directly at us.

"Now, Quandra here knows the rules. If you get here before 7 pm, there is no fee to dance. Each hour after 7 pm, the fee goes up. That is, of course, unless you get listed as the club dime. Now, the club dimes do pretty much whatever the fuck they want and the reason they get to do that is because they are the club's biggest draw. Whenever they touch the stage, the niggas flock to them like flies to shit. They make me more money."

He leaned across the table and said, "And you... Miss Lyric Sutton, certainly have the potential to be one of the club dimes." He sat back in his seat before continuing, "Now, your audition will be tonight. On stage. It's Thursday, so it's going to be a busy night for us. If they like you, you stay. If not then... clearly, you don't."

He reached his hand over to his radio and pressed play on the CD. Some house music came on as he smiled, "Now, let me see a sample."

I looked at Quandra as she nodded in my direction for me to go ahead. I turned back towards the club owner, stood up and turned around. With my hands on the chair for support, I made my ass clap right in front of him, even while I had on jeans. I saw his reaction in the mirror. His mouth dropped open as he looked at me without mercy. I saw his hand reaching up to smack it, but I turned around before he could.

"You got-damned, tease!"

He said, laughing, "But that's it. That's it right there. You tease them. Tease the fuck out of them and make them drop more of that money on the stage for you. That's it. You'll be a club dime in no time."

He looked towards LaQuandra, "Now if you ladies will please excuse me, I have some work I need to attend to. I will see you two fine, fine ass women back here tonight."

Quandra smiled and rose from her seat as she headed out of the room. I followed her close behind, and before I knew it, we were out of the strip club.

"Bitch, what I tell you? This is going to be the easiest money you've seen in forever. This shit should be illegal."

We got in the car, and she drove us to the liquor store. She said she always got drinks before she danced. It helped her loosen up, but me? I was more of a weed smoker to relax. Two blunts and I'm ready to go. Any butterflies that I had before then were just as high as me, and everything was fine. She grabbed her liquor, and we headed to the Hilton in downtown Chicago. She got us a room on the 17th floor that overlooked downtown. I could only imagine what it looked like at night. I stood, looking out the window as she came up behind me.

"This shit is beautiful, ain't it?" she asked, as she took a drink of Patron before continuing, "I always come here. This same room. I believe it has the best view of the city. I actually just stand there looking out the window like you doin' right now. I forget about shit, you know, shit I'm going through. It's peaceful, ain't it?"

I nodded my head as she took another drink and walked away. I couldn't help but think about Junie. How we always said we would tour the world and stay in expensive hotels. He had dreams for both of us to do big things, but it was all cut short. I thought getting away would get my mind completely off the tragedy and maybe it would. Maybe I just needed a little more time to be out here. I mean, I just got here, so I couldn't expect things to change magically right when I stepped foot in Chicago. Some of it would take time but time is all I had. I looked over at my suitcase and began pulling things out that I was going to wear for the night. If I was going to embrace my new life, I was going to start now. The only way I would turn back is if I felt that I had to wrap up some unfinished business. I slid a thong on as it seemingly disappeared into thin air around my waist. Suzie Rock was dying, and the woman she was becoming was unrecognizable to me.

Chapter 6

I got onto the stage. The light shined down on my face as I looked around the audience like a panoramic view. The audience glared back at me, waiting for me to do something. Say something. They had their hands in the air, cell phones up taking pictures of me and recording. I looked to my right as time seemed to slow down. Junie stood there smiling, his head nodding up and down, urging me to start. He was there. I was just happy to know that he was with me up here. I reached for the microphone, but my hand gripped the pole instead. I turned back to the audience as full grown men stood closer to the stage. The cell phones that were once in everyone's hand were now dollar bills. Their eyes undressed me even more than I already was. I looked to the right to feel the calm from Junie. He was gone. The DJ licked his lips at me and shook his head like he wanted his piece of me like every other thirsty ass nigga in the club. The high was beginning to fade, and as the house music started, I turned around, my ass facing the audience. I closed my eyes and made it clap. My audition finally began.

"Hell yeah! Bend that ass over!"

"Got-damn! Look at that shit! Let me taste it!"

I heard the same thing every night for the next week. Thirsty ass niggas coming into the club with money and lust-filled hearts just to see us shake our asses for them, hoping for something more. I wasn't complaining, though; the money was too good for me to say anything about it and I was either drunk or high as shit when I got on stage so I could numb myself to all the men and women grabbing at me. I hated that part of the job, but Quandra told me I couldn't snap back at niggas when they tried to talk to me or pull me over for a dance. I wasn't used to it because it just wasn't in my persona but, "In order to get the bees you gotta have some sweet honey to draw them in." That's what Quandra would say, so I softened my approach after the first night.

I came home with about $800 every day I went in and even though it wasn't a life I wanted, it was the life that I preferred over going back to Milwaukee. I thought about Junie from time to time. I thought about how he would feel knowing his woman is out here stripping for a living. The thing is, I don't think he would care too much about my stripping. He would be more concerned about the fact that I quit rap to do it.

"Hey, bitches, y'all need to get ya shit together and hit the stage," Don said as he walked into the back room. I paid no attention to him as he walked around as if he owned the world. I sat down and pulled singles out of my bra and G-string as naked and half-dressed women around me scattered out, leaving me alone with Don. He smiled at me, sliding his hands into his pockets as he strolled right up to me.

"This muthafucka," I mumbled under my breath as he approached.

"How is my little money maker doin'?" he asked, brushing his hand through my long, black hair.

I moved my head away from his hand and stood up.

"Shit, I would be doin' much better if you kept yo' fuckin' hands to yo'self. I get enough of that shit on the floor."

Rejection seemed to have increased his aggression. I looked into the mirror to make sure my make-up was still on point.

He walked up behind me, brushing his erect penis across my ass. A look of annoyance spread across my face, "Don, back the fuck up, damn! I'm trying to get ready."

"Oh, baby, don't be like that," he said, smiling as he smacked my ass. It jiggled on its own for a few seconds as he sat and watched in admiration. "You know, I treat you better than all these other hoes up in here. And you only been here a few days."

"Shit, is that supposed to make me feel better?"

"Nah," he said, scooting closer to me, "but I got somethin' that can."

"Shit, I hope you are talkin' 'bout yo' tongue cuz that lil piece of shit you got in yo' pants ain't doin' nothin' for me."

I walked away from him as Quandra walked into the room. She stood against the wall with her arms folded. I wasn't sure how much of our interaction she caught but the way she looked at me said she had seen enough of it. I walked past her and made my way to the floor.

"Look at that ass!"

I heard Don yell out the room as I walked down the hallway. I wasn't sure how much longer I could put up with him. The moment a nigga crossed the line when I was in Milwaukee, he quickly found out that I was the wrong chick to fuck with like that. Here, I had to practice a restraint that I never had to begin with. I was two different people, and one of them had to die for the other to live. I added a couple hundred dollars more to my total and waited for Quandra to get done with her dance so we could go back to the hotel.

***

"Damn, bitch! I see you rollin' in that bread now."

I sat on my bed, counting the money I made from dancing last night. Quandra stood next to me looking down at the bills I separated in piles.

"Shit, it takes me a couple days to pull that kind of loot. Them muthafuckas love you up there."

"I guess. I'm just trying to get this money; that's it."

I saw the smile she had on her face slowly fade away out of the corner of my eye when I turned to count the money. Her lip curled up as she peered at me. I quickly turned towards her as her smile reappeared.

"Well, shit. You are getting' it. Ain't no question about that shit."

She walked over to the dresser, "Has Don talked to you?"

"20...40...60," I paused and turned towards her, "about what?"

She combed her hair in the mirror. "The word is that he wants you to be a club dime and shit."

"Girl, I ain't thinkin' 'bout that bullshit. I'm just tryin' to get this money; that's it. He can have that club dime shit."

"I don't know. It wouldn't be any harm just to accept it. I mean, some perks come with it."

"290...300...330... Like what?"

"Shit, I don't know. I ain't no dime but from what I heard, it's just extra shit. Like guaranteed pay for slow nights, come in whenever the fuck you want. You don't have to pay him extra if you come in after 7. You know, shit like that."

She turned towards me, leaning back on the dresser. "I'll talk to him for you and set it up."

"500...510, 530, 550..."

I looked up at her just in time to see her eyeballing the money that I counted on my bed. She quickly turned back to me.

"Aight, whatever. Shit, just make sure that nigga know I ain't promising nothing," I said.

"Oh, yeah, no doubt. I'll make sure he knows that. I'll make sure he knows it one hundred percent."

She smiled and walked out of the room. Something was up with her. I noticed it, but I didn't feel a need to call her out on it. Not yet. If it wasn't for her, I wouldn't even be in the position to make this kind of money so quick, so I didn't want to jump the gun. But if I learned anything about being on the streets of Milwaukee, it's always to watch your back. Even when those you trust are behind you. There was an awkward silence between us as we rode to the club. She avoided eye contact with me, glancing out her side window periodically, but I didn't mind. I didn't want her conversation to blow my high before I got on stage. She brought me in a little early, so I could talk with Don. I wasn't thrilled about it, but I figured it couldn't hurt. As long as the nigga didn't try anything with me like he normally did, I would be aight.

I walked into his office as he closed the door behind me. I could feel his eyes scanning my body as he walked past me and motioned with his hand,

"Have a seat, baby."

I sucked my teeth and walked over to the seat by his desk. I had flashbacks of the first time I came in here with Quandra. The nervousness I felt back then was gone.

"So, Quandra tells me you want to be a club dime?"

He reclined in his seat, a crooked smile on his face.

"What? Nah. I don't care about that shit enough to want to be one."

"Well, let me rephrase that. She told me that you wouldn't mind being a club dime."

"Look, like I said, I don't give a fuck about that shit."

"You should," he said, leaning forward in his chair, "bitches in here kill for that title. I mean, it comes with protection and everything."

"Protection? The fuck I need protection for?"

He stood up and began pacing the office,

"You don't think these bitches in here haven't noticed the fact that you're coming in here and making a name for yourself in such a short time? Stealing their men and their money and taking all the attention away from them. The attention that they had in abundance before you came along."

"Ok, and what the fuck do I need protection for? These bitches in here? Please."

He stopped to look at me, then continued pacing the room. "It's not just for your protection from harm. It's for protection in case… some of your money gets stolen. You know? Things like that do happen around here."

I shook my head and rolled my eyes as he continued to pace.

"I, as the owner of this establishment, will ensure that whatever is stolen is returned to you."

"And this is only available to me as…"

"That's right. The club dime."

I looked to the right as he walked up behind me, running his hand across my arm. The anger began building inside of me as his dark, manicured fingers danced down the edges of my arm. I had the urge to smack it away, but I restrained myself and stood up.

"You know what, I'm good."

"Excuse me?" He looked surprised.

"I said I'm good. I don't need your fuckin' protection from these bitches or anything else you tryin' to offer me. I'm just here to make money and leave. I don't need any extra shit."

I turned to walk out the office as he said, "You'll change your mind soon, Ms. Lyric. I'm sure of it."

I closed the door behind me, then walked down the long hallway to the backroom. Quandra was in the mirror getting herself ready as I walked in. She smiled.

"That was quick," she said.

"What was?" I threw my things into my locker.

"The initiation process. You're a club dime now, ain't you?"

"Hell no. Fuck that shit."

The smile on her face dropped. She peered at me as I pulled clothing out of my bag.

"So, you just turned him down?"

I spun around towards her. "Yeah. Why you so worried about it?"

"Oh... just because that title is the shit these bitches live for in here. Everybody wants to be a fuckin' club dime."

"Not me. I'm good with the shit I got now."

She paused, then said, "Aight. Well, shit, I'ma go out here and see what it's lookin' like. You know today is supposed to be live. Muthafuckin' players from the Bulls is expected to be here tonight and shit, so you know it's gon' be bread out there. I'ma be back."

Her high heels clicked against the cement floor as she walked away. I stripped down and began putting on the clothes I was going to dance in. As much as I hated to admit it, I was starting to miss rap. It was easier to be myself behind a microphone than it was butt ass naked on stage. I heard a few more sets of high heels clicking against the ground, getting closer and closer to me by the second. They were coming down the hallway, talking loud and laughing as soon as they entered into the backroom.

"Hey Lyric," one of the girls said to me as she walked past. Out of the four that came in, she was the only one to speak. The others huffed and kept walking, but I didn't care. The things Don told me sat in the back of my head, but I dared any one of those bitches to try me. I had over a week of pent-up aggression that I was ready to let loose.

"It's gonna' be some ballers out there tonight, girl. I know you ready, though," she said. Then she sat down next to me, pulling a small mirror out her purse to check her makeup.

"Yeah, that's what I heard."

"If you make anything under a stack tonight, something is wrong. The way you been stackin' since you been here makes me think you been doin' this for longer than you tell everybody."

"Nah. I mean, if you got ass and titties and knew how to move them a little bit then you got a good shot at doin' this."

"I knew it," she said, slapping herself on the leg. I looked at her with a side-eye,

"Knew what?"

"I knew you sound familiar. I just couldn't put it together 'til now. 'Suzie rock the Mic like granite, muthafuckas' can't stand it.' Hell yeah, you're Suzie Rock!"

That's the last thing I wanted. I figured coming to Chicago; people wouldn't readily recognize me even knowing that Chicago was so close to Milwaukee. If anybody did notice me,

I was hoping it wouldn't be from me being in this strip club. I kept silent for a second, then,

"Nah, you must have the wrong person."

"Naw, fuck that. I know fuckin' Suzie Rock when I hear her. The fuck you doin' here?"

I slammed my locker closed and stood up, looking at myself in the mirror. The scars from my surgery were faint, blending in with my complexion but if you focused, you could see them easily.

"I told you, you got the wrong person."

She stood up next to me,

"Why are you bullshittin'? Suzie Muthafuckin' Rock. You know, I heard you for the first time when my little brother was playin' some mixtape in my car. He was like, *yo, listen to this chick*, so I listened, and you were flowin'. I was like, 'the fuck is this bitch?' you know? In a good way though cuz you were rippin' that shit."

I didn't say a word. All I could see was Junie on stage in my mind, hyping me up to keep flowing. "Spit that shit, Suzie," he would say just loud enough for me to hear him over the crowd. I had stopped the daydream before I had a chance to tear up.

"You still rapping?"

I looked at her and didn't say a word. The next thing she heard was my footsteps walking away from her down the hall. She wouldn't understand even if I told her. The club was packed when I walked outside. The club DJ spoke into the microphone when I stepped onto the floor.

"Oh wait, wait just a god-damned minute! There she is... one of the BADDEST bitches in Chicago. She wants everybody to call her Lyric, but I can't do it myself 'cause she remind me of

Diamond. Y'all, remember her from Player's Club? Hell yeah, so y'all can call her Lyric, but her ass is priceless like a Diamond. Y'all ballin' ass muthafuckas, make sure y'all get a dance or two from her beautiful ass. I can't afford her but shit, I know y'all niggas can!"

I walked through the club as a few men reached out for me. My first reaction was to jerk away from them, but I was learning. *Let them*, I said to myself as one of them pulled me in closer. I brushed my hand across his face,

"You want a dance?"

He smiled, moving his hand to touch my ass, but I smacked it away, "Nah baby, you gotta pay for that."

He pulled out a stack of money and flashed it in front of me.

"Is this enough? He asked, a twisted smile on his face.

I licked my lips seductively and pulled him up by the hand. He towered above me when he stood, and I led him to the back area where the lap dances were performed. As we walked past the security guard that stood by the entry, the man slipped something into the guard's pocket. The guard looked at it, gave a nod and then I continued to the back area with the customer. He sat down on the couch as I backed away from him. He pulled more money out of his pocket and made it rain in hundred dollar bills before I even began. At that point, I knew he would be my only customer for the night. I turned around and shook my ass slowly from left to right as I felt his hand creep up on me. I didn't mind him touching me, I mean, with that much money on the ground, I could afford him that. I backed into him, grinding on top of him as he leaned back,

"Damn, you workin' that shit."

He smacked my ass. I kept going, knowing he loved every bit of it as I spun around and put my titties on his face. I felt his dick rising while I was on top of him. I knew I was doing my job. I spun around while I was on top of him and split my legs open, leaning forward to the ground on my hands and popping my ass in his face. His hands gripped my backside and smacked me again; I felt the weight of my ass jiggle after his hand left my cheeks. I slid down to the ground and bounced my ass up and down while I was doing the splits, then made my way back up to him and went into a slow grind. Before I knew it, I felt his dick again but this time, it was outside of his pants.

I looked down, "Wait, hold on, what are you doing?"

He smiled, "I'm doing what I came here to do."

He held me with one arm and slid my panties to the side with his hand, trying to force himself inside of me. I put my hand up, shoving his face back as he grabbed me and threw me down on the couch and got on top of me.

"Stop! Stop!"

I yelled at the top of my lungs, but the music from the club drowned me out. The guard was nearby, but he didn't budge. He didn't even turn to look into the room as the man overpowered me. I struggled to break free, but it was no use. He pinned me down and slid his dick inside of me against my will.

"Stop! Please!"

Tears started falling out my eyes as he ignored me, thrusting in and out as I did all I could to shove him off of me. After a few moments, I stopped trying. It was pointless as he continued, pushing his dick deep inside of me as I laid there helpless until he was finished. A few minutes felt like hours as he finally got off of me and stood up, pulling his pants back on his waist. He took a few more hundreds out of his pocket and threw them in my face,

"There you go, bitch. That's about what that was worth."

He laughed as he walked out of the room. The guard left and followed him down the hallway, not once looking in my direction. I held my cries in as I got up and left the room, unconsciously leaving the majority of money that wasn't stuffed in my bra strap or thong on the floor. I did my best to keep my composure as I walked on the floor, making my way to the back room. I didn't see the man that just raped me, but I wasn't looking. I was walking, like a zombie, unaware of anything going on around me as I was focused on reaching my destination.

When I got to the back room, I sat on the bench and cried harder. I was broken, and it was something that I never thought I would ever experience. Not a thug ass female rapper from Milwaukee. I never allowed myself to be in a position to be treated like this until now. It wasn't until now that I knew I was out of place and didn't belong here. Moments later, I felt a hand on my shoulder. I jumped up and backed into a table, knocking make-up trays onto the floor. Don looked as if I startled him.

"Lyric. What's wrong, baby?"

I wiped tears from my eyes doing my best to conceal my pain.

"Lyric? Talk to me. Talk to Daddy. What happened?" He seemed concerned but to me, it was a charade. I didn't say anything to him as I kept my position, pinned against the table. He stepped closer, "Come on now, tell me what happened? I'll take care of it."

I remained silent, slapping his hand away from me when he reached to touch me.

"You know," he said, the concern in his voice gone, "if you went ahead and became a club dime like I told you to, maybe you wouldn't be in this position. Do you want to reconsider?"

A devilish grin flashed across his face as he stood there with his hands in his pockets. The stream of tears that I could no longer hold back fell slowly from my eyes, one after the other. My hand gripped the table I was leaning against. The pain in my heart was quickly transforming into anger as I pieced together what just happened to me, realizing that the man in front of me may have had a hand in setting it all up. He continued,

"See, it's all about protection. The club's top girls get the clubs top security. And you thought I was just talking about protection from these bitches? Oh, no, no, no, my dear. You see, all types of niggas come into this muthafuckin' club with evil intentions. Niggas that are so fuckin' narcissistic that they believe every bitch in the club wants them and when they reject them, they take offense to it. They then take the situation into their own hands as... I'm sure you just found out."

"Wait, you knew about this shit?" I asked, rage beginning to bubble inside of me.

"Knew about it? I knew it would happen eventually... if you're asking if I had a hand in it? Who's to say? I mean, I'm not the only one in this club that was after you."

He turned around and began pacing through the backroom. As soon as his attention was off of me, I grabbed an iron that was on an ironing board just to the left of me and smacked him across the head with it.

"Bitch, what the fuck?!"

He yelled as he fell to the ground, holding his head. I took the iron and smashed him across the face with it, splitting open his forehead as blood flew back into my face. He held his hands up, protecting himself against the blows as I hit him repeatedly. He screamed for help at the top of his lungs as some of the women and a security guard rushed to the back. I swung the iron at the guard as he ducked and grabbed me, tackling me to the ground not too far from where Don laid on the ground.

"That muthafucka' had me raped! Get the fuck off me!"

I screamed at the top of my lungs as Don Wallace withered on the ground in a growing pool of his own blood. The girls that ran in covered their mouths holding in vomit, as they looked at the blood spilling from Don's forehead. The guard yelled for someone to call the police as tears fell down my face while I screamed,

"He got me raped! Fuck him! I hope he dies! I hope he dies right there on that fucking ground!"

I spit in Don's direction as he covered his forehead, rolling around in his own blood. I wanted him to die and feel as much pain as he could before he did. I wanted him to feel helpless. I wanted him to feel the life draining slowly from his body as he laid there, not able to do anything about it but accept it. I wanted him to feel what it was like to be raped.

Chapter 7

They put me in a small room at the police station. I sat there stone-faced, still in shock over everything that just happened to me. They didn't know that I had been raped. They didn't even ask me. They just came to the club, looked at what I did to Don and put me in cuffs. Next thing I knew I was here in this room, alone. All I could see was the face of my attacker flashing in and out of my mind like a nightmare. A detective finally came in the room. He was tall, slim with a thin goatee that connected to his beard. His bushy eyebrows made it look as if he pushed them in the opposite direction of where they were supposed to go. He had a bad case of acne on both of his cheeks. It could have been from shaving, but I didn't look at him long enough to tell. He sat down just across from me.

"So, Miss... Lyric Sutton? I am Detective Spencer. How are you doing?"

I didn't respond.

"You don't want to talk?"

I looked away from him, staring at the wall just to his left. He sighed, sitting the pen and paper down on the table in front of him. He crossed his arms over his chest and folded his leg one over the other.

"Miss Sutton, please don't make this difficult. I just want to get your side of the story. I mean, because the other side? They're talking, and they are not modest about it."

I turned to look at him giving off a cold, hard stare. His acne was not from shaving. I turned back towards the wall.

"Miss Sutton, this is what it is. You have beaten Don Wallace to the point that his forehead was split open. Right now, you're going to be charged with assault and possibly attempted murder. Now, you can either tell me your side of the story or you can leave it as is and get whatever is coming to you."

I remained silent as tears bubbled in my eyes. I couldn't decide which emotion to act on as I sat in my seat, replaying my rape over and over. He huffed and stood up, preparing to go out of the room. Right when he reached the door, I let it out,

"He had me raped! I was taken to a back room and raped!"

He stopped and turned back towards me. "What do you mean you were raped? You were raped by Don?" He sat back down in his seat with kind eyes as he pulled his chair closer to me. "Miss Sutton, please. Who raped you?"

I wiped the tears from my eyes. "I... I was dancing for one of the men in the club. He... asked for a lap dance, you know? So I took him to the back where we normally do the dances. I saw him hand some money to the security guard. I didn't think twice about it because I'm new. I've only been working there for about a week. Well, I start dancing for him and next thing I know, he pulled his dick out and forced himself inside of me. I told him to stop, I yelled for help, but nobody came. Not the security guard. Nobody."

"Ok, Miss Sutton. You said he had you raped. Who is he?"

"Don."

"Don Wallace, had you raped? What made you say that?"

"Afterward, I went to the back where the girls dress and get ready for the show. Nobody was back there when I went in there. The club was full of ballers, so I knew it would probably be empty. Moments later, Don comes back there and he's, you know, insinuating that if I had become one of his club dimes like he offered me, none of this would have happened."

He handed me some more Kleenex. I paused for a moment, taking a deep breath before I continued.

"So I'm just sitting there thinking while he is talking like… how did he know what just happened? So, I'm just putting two and two together that me rejecting his offer to be a club dime earlier that day had something to do with it. So, I just snapped. I picked up the closest, hardest thing I could and I smacked him across the face with it until somebody pulled me off of him."

The detective leaned back in his seat, rubbing his chin. I couldn't tell if he thought I was full of shit or not but the tears that were falling from my eyes were real.

"Do you know who your attacker was?"

"No. I've never seen him before until that night. He was tall, though. Light skinned, a nappy fro. It was dark though so I can't really remember the details."

"Do you want to do a rape kit?"

"What is that?"

"They will swab you and get any DNA evidence they can so they can find out who raped you."

"No, officer. I just want this to be over. I just want to go back home and forget all this ever happened. I shouldn't have even come out here in the first place."

He stood up, visibly bothered by what I just told him. I didn't know what was going to happen next, but I just wanted to leave.

"We're going to keep you here overnight so we can sort some of this stuff out. Right now, it's just *he said she said*, and Don Wallace is ready to press charges against you for what you did to him. But before any of that, I'm going to look into this rape. If you change your mind about doing a kit, just let one of the guards know and we will get you taken care of, alright?"

"Alright."

He sighed and left the room. A few moments later, another guard came in and placed me in a holding cell. I thought it was all fucked up. I'm the one that got raped, but I was the one in jail. It didn't make sense to me, but I didn't question it. I felt like Don got what he deserved and I still wished he was dead. I sat in the cell by myself. Minutes went by like hours. Every time I heard the door open, I hoped it was detective Spencer coming in with good news, but it felt as if he would never come.

"Excuse me?" I got the attention of one of the guards. "Can you get me an ink pen and some paper, please?"

He came back with what I requested, smiling at me in a way that said he wanted my attention. I took the items from him and rolled my eyes. I had no interest in niggas, especially after what just happened to me. I didn't want anything to do with them. I went back and sat on the cold, awkward mattress and leaned against the wall. I'd been in jail before so this was nothing new to me. I didn't feel at home, but I wasn't intimidated. I wrote rap lyrics down on the paper and scribbled them out over and over. It felt as if I had to learn how to walk all over again.

That shit was wack, Lyric. You gotta come harder than that, I said to myself as I balled up paper time and time again, tossing it onto the floor. Out of frustration, I threw the notebook on the ground and laid back down on the stiff mattress. The tears flowed out of the side of my eyes again. Maybe I left rap alone for too long, I thought, maybe I'm really done with it. I turned over on my side and went to sleep.

"Baby... baby, what the fuck is wrong with you?"

I got up off my mattress and saw him standing there. He had on the same thing he was murdered in, but it was cleaned up. No blood stains, no bullet holes. Just him.

"Junie?"

"Who the fuck you think it is? Shit. It ain't the fuckin' boogie man."

I scooted back against the wall as he walked closer to me.

"Aw, come on Lyric, don't be like that. I ain't here to hurt you." He sat down on my bed. "I miss you, though. I can tell you that much. Shit ain't the same without you."

"Yeah, I... I know the feeling."

"What the fuck are you doing in here though? I mean, the fuck are you doing in Chicago?"

"I... shit, I just lost my way when you died, Junie. I mean, shit. You were my life. You were my everything. But then you just fuckin' left me."

I felt myself getting angry.

"You actin like I did that shit by choice. I didn't want to leave you. I wasn't ready to fuckin' go, but shit, it was out of my control. I couldn't do anything about it, baby; you know that. You know if I had the choice, I'd be right here with yo' ass, loving you and makin' beats for you like always."

"I know... it's just..."

"It's hard; I feel you, baby. But you gotta keep going. That shit is still in you; you haven't lost it. Yo' name is Lyric. You can't help but flow and shit." He got up and walked over to the paper that I balled up, picking one of them up and unraveling it. "Like this here... this shit here is dope. You just gotta believe in it. You gotta know that you still got it."

"But I don't, baby; I don't!" I felt my emotions getting the best of me.

"Wait, calm down, baby, just take it easy. Listen, I'm here with you, baby. I'm here, and I'll always be here. You'll never be alone, aight? Whenever you feel like it's gettin' too hard for you, just think of us. Put me on that stage with you. Put me on that page with you and just go, aight? Write the shit out of them bars like I've always known you to do. Since high school. Remember that first time you spit off the dome when I was making that beat on the table?"

I laughed, "Hell yeah, I remember that shit."

"Exactly. That's when it was easy. Remember those times because even now, it's just as easy. Maybe even easier since you've been doing it for so long."

"It's just not the same, Junie."

"Baby, just write. I'm here, aight. I'm on that paper. I'm in that ink pen. I'm guiding your hand when you write. I'm here. Just trust me, ok?"

I wiped the tears from my eyes, "Aight."

"Now, shit, I gotta get going. I love you, though, aight? Remember that shit."

"I love you too, baby."

I woke up with the paper that I balled up laying on top of me. I didn't know how much of what just happened was a dream or reality. I know that Big Mama told me that spirits are known to visit loved ones after they die. Maybe it was really him. I sat up on my bed and grabbed the ink pen that laid next to me. I took a deep breath and wrote,

Bitches thought I was done/but I'm back with the 45 in ya' back like Bone/reclaiming my throne/muthafuckas thought it was sweet/when Junie was gone/but I'm back with a new beat/Shit is hectic, but I own these streets/my name is on the block/bitches act funny/they get the Glock tucked to their dome like fitted caps.

I dropped the pen and smiled. It flowed naturally this time. I wasn't forcing it and honestly, I felt like Junie was standing right by me while I wrote it. I knew what I had to do. I was going back to Milwaukee because Chicago was not where I needed to be. Stripping was not what I needed to be doing. Not at all.

Detective Spencer came into my cell early the next morning,

"Come on; you're out."

I opened my eyes, lifting myself onto my elbows as I laid on the bed, "Huh?"

"You're free to go. I'll give you the details when we get to the other room."

I walked like a zombie down the hall, clinching the notebook paper I wrote on throughout the night. It was my new beginning, and it was birthed while I was in solitude. He took me back to the same room and pulled the chair out for me.

"Miss Sutton, we checked out your story. We went back to the club to see if there was any footage of you going to the backroom. Come to find out; all the cameras were shut off that would have ID'd the suspect. There was no evidence that you even went to the back room, but the cameras suddenly began working around the time you began to beat Don Wallace. When we questioned him about it, he said that he wasn't aware that they weren't working. When we pressed him harder, he started to fold and in the process, dropped the charges against you."

"So, he admitted to having something to do with it?"

"No, not yet. But we talked to a few of the people at the club, and one of the girls said she had faced a similar situation as you. Even though she didn't get raped, she said she was set up to be. It turns out; he has been doing this for a while. He doesn't know that we are aware these things, but we're building a case against him."

"Ok. So, what do I do?"

"You're free to go. We will be in contact with you in the future in the instance that we find your attacker—"

I cut him off, "I don't want anything else to do with this. I just want to move on, Detective. I just want to bury this shit and not look back."

"If only it was that easy," he shook his head, "if only it was that easy." He stood up, "Do you need a ride back to your home?"

I paused for a moment, looking off to the side, "Yes. I'd appreciate that."

"We'll have you back home in a moment. Sit tight."

They called a cab for me and took care of the fare. It was a long ride through the city in rush hour. It looked much different from Milwaukee. The downtown was bigger; the buildings were taller. It was something that I didn't think I would ever get used to. I grew accustomed to the small, cozy city of Milwaukee. I don't know what it was, but I just loved being there. I called Quandra a few times as I rode in the car. Her phone just kept ringing, or it went straight to voicemail. I didn't think anything of it. Knowing her, she was out fuckin' with some niggas from the city or some shit like that. It took about an hour before we finally made it to the hotel. All I wanted to do was get in the shower and relax before I found my way back to Milwaukee.

I knew Quandra was supposed to stay for a few more weeks, but I was going to convince her to take me back to Milwaukee later that night. It was only about a two-hour drive, and I had the money to front her for gas or whatever money she would lose at the club tonight by taking me. I swiped the key on the door and pushed it open. When I walked in, the room was a mess. The covers on top of the bed were thrown to the floor; the dresser drawers were halfway open. My lamp was flipped over along with the nightstand it was sitting on top of.

What the fuck? I thought as I slowly walked through the room. All of Quandra's luggage was gone. Her clothing, her makeup, everything. I didn't make sense of it until my heart dropped and I immediately began to put things together in my mind. I kept my money wrapped up in a sock, tucked far against the wall under my bed. I dropped my purse and ran to it, reaching my hand under the bed and feeling all around for it. I didn't feel anything. *No fuckin' way*, I thought to myself as I leaped up from the bed and moved to the other side, feeling in areas I may have overlooked.

"No, no! No!" I said out loud as I pulled my phone out of my purse. I called Quandra; her phone went straight to voicemail. I dialed four times back to back, and it was the same response. I threw my phone into the wall as it broke into pieces on impact. I had over $3,000 wrapped up in that sock under the bed, and it was all gone. Big Mama warned me about Quandra. I even picked up on a little bit of her shadiness earlier in the week, but I ignored it. Now, I was ass out. The only money I had was the couple hundred dollars the dude had tucked on me before he raped me. I didn't even want it; it reminded me of something I just wanted to let go of. I sat on the floor and cried out loud with my hands over my face. I couldn't believe all of this happened to me since I came to Chicago. It was just proof that I didn't need to be here. I should never have come.

I ended up catching a greyhound back to Milwaukee. It was a much longer ride than it would have been riding in a car, but it was all I had. I left everything in that hotel room. My clothes, my suitcases, everything. Anything that reminded me of this trip is what I wanted to forget about. The greyhound ticket was only $25, so I put the rest of the money in a man's hat who was performing on his saxophone close to the bus station. I don't even think he stopped to look at the amount I put in there, he just smiled and kept playing. The only thing I could reflect on during my way back to Milwaukee was rapping, but the thought of Big Tuck couldn't help but creep in my mind. Part of me still wanted him to pay for what he did to Junie. It wasn't fair to me that he was still alive while I was going through all of this without Junie. He would have wanted me to leave it alone because he knew it could end up with me being dead but I was always a hard head. I never listened to the first words of warning. It was just who I was.

I made it into Milwaukee later that evening. The city was just as grimy as it was when I left. A few crackheads tried to sell me half of a cheeseburger for 50 cents as soon as I got off the bus. Shit, it was Milwaukee though. I expected it. The bus station wasn't far from where Big Mama lived, so I took the walk.

A few people waved to me as I walked past, "Hey Suzie! Where you been?!" I waved back at them and didn't say a word. They were going to see me again but now just wasn't the right time. I started to feel appreciated again. Not like the piece of meat I was looked at as when I stepped on stage as a stripper. I thought about Quandra again. I thought about what I would do to her if I saw her again. Another person on my list that I probably should have just left alone but the anger inside me wouldn't let it go.

I finally got to Big Mama's house. Little kids were still outside playing as it wasn't too late in the evening when I showed up. Cars still sped down the block without slowing down for the sake of the children. *Some things never change*, I thought to myself as I walked up the cement steps to the house. I didn't have my keys, so I rang the doorbell and waited for a few moments. She eventually came to the door.

"Now, who is ringing my bell this time of night?"

I could hear her fussy voice on the other side of the door. I smiled as I listened to the latches unlock. When she opened the door, she was in her nightgown with her hair wrapped up in a scarf.

"Now who—"

She paused, getting a good look at me as she flickered on the porch light.

"Lyric? Oh my God, baby, Lyric! Is that you?"

"I've been praying for you, baby. I've been praying for you mightily!" She quickly opened the door and put her arms around me tight.

I embraced her back as silent tears fell down my face. It felt good to have her arms around me. To feel the love from somebody, you knew loved you unconditionally. I imagined that she thought I really wouldn't come back and maybe she was prepared for it. She had a good reason to think that way because we barely spoke to each other since I went to Chicago. I was stripping, and it was something in me that made me believe she would just know that's what I was doing out there. She slept early, and I worked late, so I used that as an excuse the few times we did talk, and I rushed her off the phone.

"Big Ma, I know you gotta go to sleep, and I'm about to step out for a bit. I'll talk to you later, ok? I love you," and I would hang up before she could give any rebuttal. I was just calling her to let her know I was still alive because I knew how she worried. I was back home now, though. Back where I belonged, and shit wasn't going to be like it was when I left. I was hungry. Hungry to reclaim my throne as the best female emcee and hungry for revenge and no matter what, I wasn't going to stop until I was full.

Chapter 8

That night, I slept much longer than I normally did. I thought the trauma of Junie's death would have been removed from me by now, but it was still there. I woke up periodically, sweat dripping from my forehead because of nightmares. I kept replaying Junie's death over and over, which made me want to go after Big Tuck even more. I heard Big Ma walk into my room a couple of times to check on me. She regularly woke me up whenever she felt I was sleeping too long, but this time, she just let me rest. I appreciated that. I looked over at my clock when I finally rose from my bed, 12:47 pm. I felt sluggish when I got up. It seemed as if I was wrestling with something all night as parts of my body ached to no end. I slowly got out of my bed and crept down the hallway.

"Big Mama?"

I called out for her, but the house was bone silent. In the kitchen, a plate of scrambled eggs, bacon, toast, and pancakes sat on the stove covered in Saran wrap. It still had a bit of warmth coming from it, so I knew she cooked it not too long ago.

"Big Ma?"

Still nothing. I checked her room, and it was spotless. The bed was made up, dresser was spotless, and the floor had vacuum marks laid across it perfectly. She usually got up at the crack of dawn and had the house clean by 8 am.

"Girl, you stay in the bed and sleep. By the time you get up, half the work is done."

I remembered her fussing at me when I tried to sleep in on weekends in high school. She hadn't done it much these days since I got out the hospital but I knew it was just her showing compassion. All I had to do was give it a couple of months, and I knew I'd hear her voice telling me to get up earlier than I wanted to. I walked back into the kitchen and uncovered the plate. One thing I missed when I was gone was the home cooking. Big Ma didn't play in the kitchen. She tried to show me the way around in there, but I wasn't interested. Not in the least.

I finished my plate and headed into the front room dressed in a wife beater and sweats. The sun beamed down through the curtains, and a slight breeze blew into the front room. Days like this, I usually went out on the porch and relaxed. Listening to little kids run up and down the street playing, wishing that I was that age again, but these days I didn't feel like doing much reminiscing. My mind always went back to Junie's death, and it seemed that was as far back as it could go. I had flipped through the channels before I heard a knock at the door. Shaunie and Vinny stood on the other side as I peeked out the window.

"Oh, shit. Look who it is."

Vinny smiled, "What the fuck is up, nigga? Shit. I ain't even know you were back. Can't you holla at a nigga? Whassup?"

Shaunie chimed in, "You know what I'm sayin'. If it wasn't for Big Mama, we wouldn't have even known you were back. Muthafuckas go out of town without tellin' anybody and then pop back up like it ain't shit."

I stepped out onto the porch, shaking hands with both of them, "Nah, it ain't like that. I just had to roll out, you know? Shit was gettin' hard here for me."

We all took a spot on the porch and sat down as Vinny spoke up, "Yeah, I feel you. I know that shit with Junie was fucked up. And then yo' ass was in the hospital. We thought you wasn't gon' make it out and shit."

"Nah, I'm here."

"Yeah, I see. Shit. It ain't been the same without you here, though. Muthafuckas were like, *yo, where Suzie at? Where she at? That's you, guy, ain't it?* I was like, *yeah* and shit, you know? But I didn't even know what to tell them. Shit, I didn't even know where yo' ass was at."

"My bad, Shaunie. I just had to get away. I was in Chicago for a minute."

"The fuck was you doin' in Chicago?"

"Some dumb ass shit that I never should've been a part of. I went with Quandra's old thieving ass."

Vinny's mouth hung open and he said, "You went with Quandra? The big booty stripper hoe?"

"Yeah. Her ass."

"Fuck. I can't believe you went with her. She is known for doing shady ass shit. The fuck you get caught up with her for anyway?"

I looked off to the right as a little boy sped down the block on his bicycle. Two small boys were running as fast as they could after him.

"Yeah. I was just... I don't know, shit. I was desperate to get the fuck out of Milwaukee for a minute."

"I feel you."

Vinny looked towards Shaunie and shook his head, then looked back towards me, "You know Remy been talkin' mad shit since you got shot up, right?"

"Fuck you mean?"

"Remy. Shit, she was talkin' 'bout how you was soft and shit, and you were the reason Junie got shot up."

I stood up and looked directly at Vinny. "On was she sayin' that shit? Since when?"

"Since a little after you went to the hospital."

"Why the fuck you just now tellin' me?"

"Because, Lyric. Yo' ass was recovering and shit. I knew you was gon' try to go out there and find her ass but you could barely fuckin' walk. I didn't want to bring that shit to you."

"Nah, fuck that, Vinny. Fuck that."

He looked as Shaunie, "I knew I shouldn't have told her ass."

"Shaunie, you knew too?" She remained silent as the same boys that ran down the sidewalk reversed and ran past us in the other direction. I asked them again,

"She still be over at Questions?"

Both of them kept quiet.

"I swear to God y'all betta' start talkin'."

"Yeah man," Shaunie spoke up, "she's still over there. Matter of fact, they havin' some kinda battle that she is supposed to be in this Friday."

"Oh, word? Aight. Yeah, I'ma be there then. Shit. Milwaukee thought it was sweet and shit when I was gone, but they gon' be in for a rude awakening when these hoes see what's really good."

Big Mama's car pulled into the driveway as I stood there, pounding my hands together as I spoke to them. I relaxed as she got out of the car. I didn't want her to see me worked up because I knew she would question me about it later. She said I had the same attitude as Mama and Mama got it from her, so she did her best to stop the storm before it came.

"I see you finally rolled your lazy behind out of bed."

"Yeah, Big Mama. I was just tired from the trip."

She smiled, "Ummm-hmmm, I bet."

She looked towards Shaunie and Vinny, "Hey, y'all two. Are y'all stayin' out of trouble?"

They answered at the same time. "Yes, Ma'am!"

"Good, good. That's what I like to hear." She turned towards me. "Lyric, baby, I need to talk to you for a minute after you're done with your friends here."

"Ok, Big Mama, I'll be in there in a second."

She smiled and walked inside the house. I waited until she cleared the front room before I spoke to them again,

"Y'all said Friday, huh?"

Vinny huffed, "Yeah, man. Friday."

"Y'all rolling?"

Vinny spoke up first, "Shit. I gotta work."

I looked at Shaunie, who shrugged.

"I'll roll with you. Remy ass is all talk anyway. She wasn't doing shit when you was out here walkin' around and shit. She waited until you got shot up before she started poppin' off at the mouth."

"I know. She gon' get what's comin' to her, though, I guarantee that."

They got up, and I shook both of their hands before they walked off the porch. *I can't believe this shit*, I thought as I walked into the house looking for Big Ma. I found her in her room sitting on her bed, her bible open with her highlighter in her hand. I sat and waited until she was finished. She trained me never to interrupt her while she was reading or praying, unless I was dying or something was on fire. I leaned against the dresser and waited for her to get done. As I waited, I gazed at her. The wrinkles on her face began to show a bit more. The crow's feet on the side of her eyes were more visible now than they were before. Her gray eyes seemed to resemble dark clouds more than the silver lining that clouds have in front of sunshine. She put her highlighter down and closed her bible, staring at me with eyes full of grief.

"Big Ma, what's wrong?"

She tapped the space next to her on her bed without saying a word. I occupied the space as she reached over and grabbed my hand, clenching it tightly. I looked down at the wrinkles on her hand, her light skin making the blue veins completely visible. I didn't rush her to speak. On her dresser, there was a picture of her and my Grandad. He passed away when I was 19, and he was the only example of a man I had in my life. Big Ma said I got my heart from him. The strong-willed part of it. The way I didn't back away from challenges or a fight and never gave up. Just thinking about that made me regret leaving Milwaukee in the first place.

"I had a doctor's appointment today," she finally spoke.

I felt my stomach turn.

"I had a lump in my breast for quite some time, but I never got it checked out. I figured it would go away on its own, you know?"

Tears began to form in my eyes, but I turned my head away from her.

"Turns out, it's cancer."

I shook my head slowly from left to right in disbelief of what I was hearing. I turned towards her and not a single tear was in her eyes.

"Now, baby, it's not the end. Ok? I don't want you to think that it's the end. This is a new chapter in Big Mama's life, ok?"

Tears fell out of my eyes in streams, "What do you mean, Big Mama?"

"I'm taking chemotherapy. I start tomorrow, and it's going to help me in the process."

"Big Mama, no. No, this can't be happening right now."

I bent over and covered my face as the tears fell from my eyes like April rain. She reached over and put her arms around me. I heard her sniffle, but she tried to keep it hidden the best she could.

"Baby, Big Mama is gonna be alright, ok? The Lord knows what's best, and if this is the path He has chosen for me then this is the path I'm going to walk down, hear?"

I responded in tears as she squeezed me tighter.

"Big Mama is going to be ok, Lyric. Alright? Big Mama is going to be ok."

I raised my head up. "Big Mama, what am I going to do if you're not, though, huh? What am I going to do? I don't have anybody else left here. It's just you."

Her face was filled with sorrow that wasn't there when we first began talking. I believe it was more because of my reaction than the Doctor's diagnosis.

"Baby, you have the good Lord here. He will never leave you or forsake you; you gotta know that, alright? You gotta know that."

I buried my head into her chest and cried harder. What she was saying was going in one ear and out the other. It wasn't that I didn't believe in the Lord, it was just that I couldn't believe that He would allow this to happen. I couldn't fix my mind to think that she would be all right, and the faith that she had was not in me. I put my arms around her and held her tight like I could keep her in this spot forever. Like my squeeze would keep cancer in one place and not progress. It was all make believe, though, and no matter how I looked at it, it felt like the Lord was picking on me. He was rapidly taking away the people that were crutches in my life, and it was that moment that my resentment began. As my head rested on her chest, I felt her tear splash onto the back of my neck. It was at that moment that I believe she knew her life was coming to an end, and it broke my heart even more.

Chapter 9

Friday came faster than I expected. I was helping Big Mama around the house so much that she almost had to push me away from her.

"Girl, get on outta here! I don't need you to feed me! I'm sick, but I can still work my limbs." She waved her arm as if she was going to swing at me. "Now get on out of here! You got places you need to be!"

"Big Mama, I'm not going anywhere."

"Why not?"

"I need to stay here with you."

"No, you don't! Stop smothering me! Girl, get on out this house and have fun with your friends! You just make sure you're careful. I need you back here in once piece!"

I laughed, "Big Mama, I'm just trying to make sure you're alright."

"Baby, you've done plenty! You've been cooking for me, and you've been up cleaning this house before I could even get up myself. Big Mama appreciates that, but now, you're smothering me! Get on out of here before you drive me crazy!"

I laughed and kissed her on the forehead before I left her in her room. She already started losing her hair from the chemotherapy, but I showed her how to tie a bandanna around her head fashionably. It was incredible to me how she kept her strength through it all. That bible stayed near her, even in the midst of the sickness she was facing. It said a lot about who she was and the God she served, but it didn't resonate with me. I was still angry that He even allowed it to come to this.

Big Mama had gotten me a new phone to replace the one I broke. I told her I dropped it when I was getting off the greyhound, and it shattered. She still didn't know that I had been raped in Chicago. Nobody knew. I just wanted to bury it along with everything else that happened while I was there. It only took me a little while to get ready. I threw on some tight jeans, a fitted t-shirt, and a snapback. I wasn't trying to be fancy, but I still wanted to make sure I had everyone's attention. I walked back into Big Mama's room to check on her before I left. Just that fast, she was sound asleep. I took her plate off her table and kissed her on the forehead. I started to tear up, but I controlled myself, not giving them the chance to fall.

Shaunie was already outside waiting for me when I stepped on the porch. I took a deep breath and walked to the car.

"You ready?" She asked.

"Yup. Let's go."

The club was deep in the hood on Milwaukee's north side. The line was already stretching out the door when we showed up. Women dressed in skimpy dresses and short skirts were scattered throughout the line as men crowded around them like vultures.

"I'm not tryin' to wait in line."

"Shit, what you wanna do then?"

I looked at the line again, "Drive around to the back."

We drove past the club and went down the alley to the back of the club. Two men stood outside guarding the entrance when I got out. I was hoping Block, one of the guys I had known before I stopped rapping, would be on the door. Everybody called him Block because of how big he was. His shoulders were wide as a city block, and he was built like one as well. He flicked his cigarette to the side as I walked up to the door.

"Aye," he said in a deep, calloused voice, "this entry ain't for y'all. I don't give a fuck how thick you is."

I walked up closer, moving from out of the shadows and standing under the dim light that hung atop of the back door.

"Suzie? Oh, shit. Suzie Muthafuckin' Rock."

"What up, Block?"

"Shit."

He shook hands with me and said, "Where the fuck you been?"

"I been around."

"You ain't been around here. Muthafuckas ain't seen you since Junie ass got popped, RIP."

"Yeah, I know. I had to take some time away from shit and cool down."

"I feel you. So, what's up? You tryin' to get in?"

"Yeah. I'm good for it?"

"You know you good for it. Just have yo' gal park the car in that lot, though. She can't leave that shit right there... with her fine ass."

Shaunie got back into the car and moved it down to the parking lot not too far from the door.

"Remy here?"

"Nah, not yet. You must've heard what she said about you."

"Hell yeah, you know what I'm sayin'. I just wanna set some shit straight tonight."

"I feel you but aye, I'm lettin' you in this muthafucka so don't go in there causin' no shit, though."

"Block, you know me."

"Exactly. Why the fuck you think I said that?"

Shaunie walked back up to us as we stood in front of the door. Block looked at her like he was interested but too shy to say anything to her. He stood to the side and opened the door for us to walk in. As Shaunie walked a few feet in front of me, I whispered in his ear.

"I'll put in a word for you, bro."

"My nigga."

He said as he shook my hand with a big kool-aid smile plastered across his face.

We walked down the back hallway as we heard a crowded building in the front. I didn't want to go out there because I didn't want anybody to notice me until I did what I came to do. I stopped as Shaunie was making her way out to the front. She turned to look at me.

"Whassup?"

"I'ma chill back here for now."

"Ok."

She cracked the door open that led to the front, watching the crowd fill the room.

"Well, I'ma chill out there and shit. I'm slayin' too hard to be chillin' in the back unseen."

I laughed, "Aight, that's cool."

"When you ready to go, just let me know."

"Aight."

She went out the door as I stayed in the back, looking for an area to chill until the show started. Moments later, Block came down the hall.

"Block?"

"Whassup?"

I looked around, almost hesitant to ask him, "Is Big Tuck still around here?"

"Yeah. Tuck still be around. Why?" He looked at me with a cold stare.

"I'm just askin'."

"I hope that's all you doin' is just askin'. Don't fuck with that nigga, Suz. It's death all over that."

I brushed him off, "Thanks, Block."

He shook his head and walked down the hallway as I faded back to the spot I was in. Everybody in the city had Big Tuck as this untouchable muthafucka', but I knew there was a way to him. There had to be. Every man, no matter how powerful he is, has his weakness. Sometimes, it just takes a little digging to find out what it is. I sat in one of the back rooms on a stool, leaning against the wall. I could clearly see the back door and everybody who came through it. It wasn't much longer before Remy came in.

She had a look on her face as if she owned the world. She was dark skinned; long, black hair hung down to the middle of her back. The gloss on her lips shined bright under the dim lights as she walked down the hallway with a handful of people. She didn't notice me tucked away in the corner as I stayed in my seat, watching her moves. *This bitch*, I thought, wanting to confront her right there but I restrained myself. They walked past the room I was in and went a little further down the hallway. I felt Junie sitting in the room with me, urging me to do what I came to do.

"Rip that shit up, Lyric. Rip it the fuck up."

It wasn't long until I heard them call her to the stage. The crowd cheered for her as I crept out of my room, Junie right behind me. Block walked past and I grabbed his arm.

"Aye, let me get on stage."

"Let you get on stage?"

He asked like it was the craziest thing in the world. "You gon' have me fuck around and lose my job with that shit, Suzie."

"Trust me, Block. Muthafuckas are gonna be talkin' about this shit for months. Just make sure I get on stage uninterrupted. That's it. Please, Block."

"Aight Suzie, damn! You better be doin' some epic ass shit for this! Fuck!" He sighed as he loomed in front of me, seemingly tall enough to brush the ceiling with his head.

I threw my arms around him. "Thank you, Block! Oh, one more thing… can you get me a mic?"

"God-damn, Lyric! You askin' for a lot!"

"Last thing, I promise. I'll remember you for this."

"Remember me by hookin' me up with yo' fat booty ass friend."

"Consider it done."

"Yeah, yeah… look, when you tryin' to do this shit?"

"As soon as possible."

He looked up and down the hallway. "Aight, come on, shit. We are going now."

We walked down the hallway and made our way to the stairs at the back of the stage. If Block wasn't with me, I would've been stopped well before I got this far. Remy was on stage in the middle of her verse as we stood on the bottom step. The crowd was into it as my heart began racing like it was the first time I started rapping. My mind flashed back to high school when I was at the lunch table, the first time I freestyled in front of Junie and his friends. I remembered the feeling I had after I was done and how everybody went crazy over what I said. I saw Junie's smile. The dimples that pushed his cheeks all the way in. His earrings sparkling like his smile.

The nostalgia swept over me as Block handed me the microphone. It felt like that was the thing that gave me all the confidence I needed. I walked up the steps and in moments, I was on stage behind Remy. The crowd grew silent as Remy kept rapping, looking around as if something happened to change the energy in the room. Remy put the mic down and looked behind her as the crowd began to recognize the same thing she did. It was bone silent for a few moments as the DJ stopped the music.

Suddenly, the crowd erupted, "Suzie!" They yelled my name as she took another step back.

"Hold up, what the fuck is she doing here?"

Her eyes widened, but she quickly let them fall back into place to hide her nervousness. By that time, it was too late. I already smelled the blood in the water.

"Yeah bitch, you thought I was done, huh?"

"The fuck? Somebody get this bitch off the stage."

I looked towards the back as Block stood there, controlling the scene. I smiled. I had all the time I needed as she took a step away from me. The crowd went crazy as I stepped closer to the front of the stage,

"Yo, DJ, can you bring that beat back?"

"Nah, don't do shit!" Remy snapped, but I turned towards the DJ, smiling the way I did when I wanted to convince Junie to do something for me. Suddenly, the beat came back. I looked at Remy,

"I'm about to murder you on yo' own beat, bitch."

The crowd went crazy, cheering me on as I started.

"Bitches thought I was done/but I'm back with the 45 in ya' back like Bone/reclaiming my throne/muthafuckas thought it was sweet/when Junie was gone/but I'm back with a new beat/Shit is hectic, but I own these streets/my name is on the block/bitches act funny/they get the Glock tucked to their dome like fitted caps…"

She stormed off the stage and went to the back as I rapped for a little longer and exited myself.

The DJ took over the mic. "That was some shit!"

I left the crowd and went to the back where I heard Remy yelling. I stood right by her door as security stood in front of me.

Block was just to my right as I yelled in the room, "What you gotta' say now, bitch?! I'm here! What did you say about Junie? I got Junie killed? Come tell me what you said out yo' dirty ass mouth, bitch!"

"Fuck you!" She walked over to the door, but security stayed between us. "Fuck you and all the shit you talkin'! This my set! This my city, bitch! You old news!"

"Old news? Shit, I'm the reason why they are fuckin' yellin' right now."

"You gon' get yours, bitch! I swear to fuckin' God, you gon' get yours!"

I reached through her security guards, trying to grab her but they pushed me back. Block came in and pushed them off of me with a warning.

"Don't put yo' hands on her."

"She needs to stay her ass over there then."

"It's cool, bitch. Just know that yo' fans just became my fans."

"Fuck you!"

I laughed and walked away. I didn't do everything I came to do, but half of it was all right with me. I made my reappearance in my city. Everybody knew I was back now, and that was all that mattered. All the weak ass shit that was going around about me was gon' be put to rest.

"Yo, that shit was dope," someone said from the hallway. It was the DJ that was on stage when I went out there.

"Thank you. And thank you for pickin' up that beat again."

"No doubt."

As he stood under the hallway light, there was something familiar about him. Remy's yells could still be heard down the hall as I examined the man that stood in front of me. I just couldn't put my finger on it, but I had to have known him from somewhere.

"I think I recognize you."

He smiled, his dimples pushed his cheeks all the way in.

"Really? I don't believe you do."

"I mean, you... I don't know; it's just something about you that makes me feel like I've met you before."

"Nah. I know for a fact I've never met you. I just moved here from Cleveland a few months ago."

"Really? Like, I haven't seen you at a show before or anything?"

"Nah," he laughed, "I don't even know who you are. This is my first time hearing you."

I tilted my head as if I was trying to piece together where I knew him from. Like he didn't know where he has been or who he has met for himself.

"If you say so."

"I know so."

"Ok. Well, thanks again."

"No problem."

It was his smile. His dimples. His demeanor. The fact that he was a DJ. All of it reminded me of Junie. Maybe that was it. It reminded me of him so much that my mind put Junie in his place. That was the only explanation for it. He turned to walk away, but I wasn't done.

"Excuse me."

He turned around.

"I'm lookin' for a DJ. I know you fuckin' with Remy and everything—"

He cut me off, "Shit, not after tonight. I know she ain't fuckin' with me after I just froze her ass out on stage. What I did was like a dog bitin' its owner's hand. Not sayin' I'm a dog or whatever, just the analogy."

"Nah, I feel you. But, I'm sayin' if you have the time…"

He smiled and handed me his card. "Yeah, you know what I'm sayin'. Just hit me up and we can um… talk a little more about it."

"I will."

He walked down the hallway as I held his card in my hand, smiling like a school girl. Many guys have tried to talk to me since Junie passed almost six months ago, but I never gave them the time of day. He was different, though. It almost felt like I was talking to Junie while he was in front of me. I looked down at his card: *Nasir Jones; producer extraordinaire*.

Chapter 10

"Hello?"

"Who this?"

"Suzie Rock."

"Suzie…?"

He paused for a moment. "Oh, right. The rapper from the other day? Right! What's up?"

"Nothin… I was just seein' what was good with you?"

"Oh, no doubt. I'm good. Most definitely."

"I was thinkin'… maybe we could get together and talk about that producing thing I brought up."

"Word. Yeah, that's cool. We can do that, fa sho. When you tryin' to get together?"

"Ummm… later on, today is cool."

"Aight, bet. Later on, it is then. I'll hit you up. Maybe we can just kick it at the mall or get somethin' to eat or some shit like that."

"Cool. I'll hit you up in a minute."

"Aight."

I would be lying if I said I didn't have butterflies when we spoke on the phone. It was a feeling he gave me that made me feel like I was melting as he was talking to me. It was almost 8 months since Junie's death and the similarities between the two of them were too strong for me just to ignore them. Honestly, if it wasn't for Junie, I may have never even looked at Nasir in that way. I'd done another show since I first came back out on the scene and fucked up Remy's spot. The ball was rolling, and I was a fool to think that it wouldn't pick up again where I left off.

Big Mama was still at the house with me. I could tell she was getting worse, but it was something she would never admit to me. Not even in the slightest way. I tossed my phone on the bed and went to the room to check on her. She was sound asleep; her head scarf wrapped tightly around her head. She didn't look as young as she used to anymore. The doctors said she had an aggressive form of malignant breast cancer. I knew it wouldn't be long before they put her in the hospital, but for now, she was staying home. It was sad watching her slowly deteriorate before my eyes. Her cheekbones were beginning to show, her eye sockets were bulging out a little more than normal. Even with all that, her bible stayed on her nightstand like it was the one thing that could keep her alive. She never lost faith. I didn't understand it, but it made me even more curious about the God she served.

The doorbell rang, moving me to leave my daydreams and see who was on the other side of the door. As I opened it, he stood there on the other end with a bouquet of roses in his hand and a card. I shook my head. It was my last resort. I didn't want to hire anybody to come out here and stay with Big Mama whenever I had to leave, so Uncle Stew was the next best thing. Big Mama kicked him out of the house over 15 years ago because he was strung out on crack and selling everything in the house he could move out on his own. From what Big Mama told me, he cleaned himself up and had been sober for the last three years, but he never forgave her for putting him out when he was struggling. It wasn't until he learned that she was sick that he was willing to come back around. He agreed to come over to stay for a few hours during the times I had to leave.

He took his hat off, exposing his freshly shaved head. His beard was lined as if he just left the barber shop. A strong gust of wind blew against the house, causing him to move just a little to the left. He smiled,

"Hey, Lyric. Girl, you lookin' more and more like yo' mama every day!"

"Whassup, Stew?"

"Can I come in?"

I moved to the side as he took a step into the house. It was his first time being there that I knew about. He looked around like he was reminiscing about how things used to be. I shut the door and walked in front of him and said,

"Stew?"

"Yes, ma'am."

"Look, we ain't here for none of yo' bullshit, aight? Now, Big Mama trusted you to come—"

He cut me off. "Lyric, sweetheart. Trust me. I'm not that way anymore. My mother is dying of cancer, and we already left on bad terms the first time. I'm just here to make things right and hopefully... make her days here as peaceful as possible. That's it."

I looked at him slowly from head to toe. If he was lying, he was doing a good job at it.

"Follow me."

He trailed behind me as we walked back to Big Mama's room. Her eyes opened as soon as we entered into her room. She tried to raise up in her bed as I rushed to her aid.

"Hold on, Big Mama. I got you."

She coughed, then looked towards Uncle Stew. Her smile was that of comfort. Like she was relieved to see him after all these years.

"Stewart? Is that you?"

He walked closer to her bed. "Yes, Mama, it's me."

I could see the tears building under her convex eyes. A stream of water under the gray clouds.

"Come here and give yo' mama a hug."

She reached her arms for him as he walked over to her. They embraced for a while as I stood there, watching them. Big Mama cried, but I guess Uncle Stew wasn't the type to just cry in front of anyone. He quickly wiped his eye when he glanced up at me. Big Mama finally let him go as he handed her the flowers.

"Here Mama. These are for you."

She gingerly took the flowers from him, her hand faintly shaking as if she was going to drop them. I reached to grab them from her.

"Wait a minute, girl!" she snapped. "I just want to smell them first." She inhaled slowly, smiling the whole time. "They smell lovely, Stewart. They are perfect."

She handed them to me as I placed them in a vase and set it next to her bible on the nightstand.

"Well, back up, boy. Let me get a good look at you."

Uncle Stew stood up and spun around for her.

"Ummm-hmmm! My baby is done cleaned himself up! Praise God!"

"Yes, Ma'am. For good, too. It's for good this time."

"I know it is."

I walked over to Big Mama, and placed my hand on her head. "I'm going to head out for a few hours, ok Big Mama?"

"Alright, baby."

"If you need anything. Anything, Big Ma, you just call me, and I'll be right back, ok?"

"Girl—" She began coughing. A loud cough that didn't seem as if it was going to end. I stood up, but she pulled me back down and held up one finger. "Girl, you get on out of here! I told you about that! You live your life. Big Mama is going to be fine, you hear?"

I wanted to believe her. I wanted to find that she wasn't deteriorating before my eyes or that every time she coughed, it wasn't a sign of the end for her. I just couldn't. I smiled.

"I love you, big Mama."

"I love you too, sugar. I'll see you later, ok? You be careful out there."

"I will."

I tapped Uncle Stew on the leg and motioned for him to follow me into the hallway. I led him to the front room, far away from Big Mama's ears.

"I'ma tell you this once and one time only. If you do *anything* to Big Mama or this house while I'm gone, you betta pray that I don't see you again."

He put his hand up to stop me from talking and said, "Listen, Lyric. I already told you that I'm clean. That's not me anymore. I love my Mama, and I always have. I was just sick before, you know? You know what it's like to be sick? To be addicted to poison? That's what I was. That's what yo' mama was. Hell, that's even what you were as a baby, but I saw my sister die with a fuckin' needle in her arm."

He leaned in closer to me.

"I saw the life leave her body. I saw that shit with my own eyes and to this day, my mind keeps telling me that it's a dream. Trying to convince me that it never happened but I see her fuckin' grave every got-damned day. Every day! I know it's real, and I know I'm not the same person. If you don't believe me, and you're just waiting for me to flip into the person I was, then pull up a chair because you're going to be waiting a long fucking time for it to happen."

I believed him. He became teary eyed while he spoke and the passion he evoked wouldn't allow me to think otherwise.

"Aight, Stew. Aight."

"Now, if you'll excuse me, I would like to tend to my Mama while I still can."

He turned and walked away, wiping his eyes dry in the process. I wanted to snap back at him but I couldn't. The truth is, he brought feelings of guilt in my heart. For the longest time, I blamed my mama for leaving me here by myself. I realized that I had the same type of bitterness about her that Uncle Stew had towards his mama. The reasons were different, but the bitterness was there none the less. I grabbed my jacket from the room and left the house.

***

We ended up meeting by the lakefront. It was a dirty ass beach with dirty ass water that nobody ever stepped foot on or in. People just came down there and parked in the parking lots blasting their music while ratchet ass chicks danced on the trunks and hoods of cars. Other people walked up and down the strip being loud for no ass reason. Muthafuckas in Milwaukee didn't have shit else to do but this. It was cool most times before the police showed up or somebody pulled out and started shooting shit up because of some beef. I took him to a spot away from all the noise. There was a walkway that led to the water. We sat down on a bench as the sun was just beginning to fall down from the sky.

"This is a nice ass spot."

I smiled. "Yeah. I had to pull you away from all that loud-ass ratchet shit that be goin' on down there."

"Shit, I'm used to that, though. Where I'm from, niggas be wildin' out all the time." He turned to look.

"Where you from again?"

"Cleveland."

I laughed, "Cleveland? What the fuck goes on in Cleveland?"

"Apparently the same shit that goes on in Milwaukee."

"I guess."

I turned and caught him looking at me, but he quickly averted his eyes, staring off into the horizon. At least I knew I had his attention.

"So, why you come to Milwaukee?"

He leaned back on the bench and folded his arms over his chest before answering. "Let's just say it's for business."

"Like, making music?"

"Hell Nah. I mean, I do that shit, but that's not why I came here."

"What kind of business then, nigga? Damn. Why are you bein all secretive?"

"The same reason you are so fuckin' nosey!"

If I closed my eyes, there was nothing in the world that would convince me that I wasn't sitting here talking to Junie. The sun dipped down lower as a couple walked by us and sat down on another bench. They were cuddled up with each other, kissing and holding hands. They looked to be about the same age as us, but it was hard to tell. I wouldn't have minded Nasir reaching in to do the same thing with me. He made me feel like a woman. Like I could pull down my outer shell and just be feminine. The same way Junie made me feel.

"What's over there?" he asked, pointing to the right. The area was off to the side, sort of secluded from the rest of the lakefront in a cul-de-sac.

"Oh, that ain't shit but some artwork that people painted on the walls. You wanna check it out?"

"Yeah, let's go check it out."

We walked further away from everybody, down the winding path until we got to the towers that marked the entrance to the temporary arts exhibit. There were paintings and drawings of all kinds of abstract things that would take forever just to find the meaning of.

"This shit is dope," he said, running his hand across the wall of paintings.

"I'm not really into art that much."

"Word? I figured the shit was connected. Like, you as a rapper would just be into this kinda shit."

"Nah, not really."

He looked back in the direction that we walked from. Nobody was coming our way. He turned back towards me and moved in closer. I stepped back.

"What you doin'?

He smiled, "What *you* doin'?"

His dimples lured me in as he bent down to me, pressing his lips against mine. It was perfect. It was Junie. I put my hands on his chest.

"Wait."

He backed up. "What? My bad, I just thought—"

I kissed him on his lips before he could finish. He smiled at me, his lips just out of reach of mine. He kissed me again, slowly as he ran his hand through my hair. I closed my eyes and let him do whatever he wanted. We could hear cars zooming by on the busy street just off in the distance, but that didn't stop either of us. He put his hands on my breasts as he backed me against the wall. His hands went down to my belt, loosening it and causing my pants to hit the floor. His hand moved over my vagina, moving his fingers back and forth against its lips. I reached for his dick, feeling the hardness and almost begging him to put it inside me. I looked to the left as the lights on the path lit up. I still couldn't see anybody coming, but I didn't care if they were.

This was our moment. I pulled his pants down, and he guided my head down to his dick as I sucked the tip of it slowly, then put it all in my mouth. His moans mixed with the noise from the cars that sped by turned me on even more. It was the allure of being caught. The chance that, at any moment, somebody could walk into the art exhibit and see us fucking. He pulled me up and turned me around, putting his dick all the way inside of me. He smacked my ass as he went in harder, deeper. He pulled my hair as I arched my back so he could go in deeper. I wanted him inside me. I wanted Junie to fuck me again like he used to.

"Fuck," I said out loud as he went in even deeper, smacking my ass harder than before. I felt the waves he made as his abs slammed against me. I reached behind and pulled him in closer to me. *Zoom! Zoom!* Two more cars sped by as he moved in and out of me with the rhythm of the ocean that was just beyond us. The sun's last rays stretched across the sky as I felt him cum inside of me. I didn't care. I didn't want him to stop. I wanted Junie's baby.

"Oh my god, are they fuckin?"

We paused when we heard the voice but when we turned to look; nobody was there. He gripped my ass and kept going as he thrust himself in one last time and it was that last one that made me cum with him. I held in my scream by biting my lip as my cum dripped slowly down my leg. I couldn't believe we just fucked in public. I'd never done it before until now, but this is the shit that made me love Junie. I opened my eyes as Nasir stood in front of me. He smiled, as he pulled his pants up.

"You ready to go, baby?"

I smiled.

"Hell yeah, I'm ready."

Chapter 11

A few weeks passed since I started kicking it with Nasir. Uncle Stew moved in permanently with us, and I didn't have a problem with it. He cooked, kept the house clean, and Big Mama didn't have any problems with him being there so I figured I shouldn't either. Her cancer had grown worse, though. The chemotherapy didn't seem to be working.

"Unc, we're gonna have to take her to the hospital."

He wiped a tear from his eye. "Yeah. Yeah, I know."

We both stood in the hallway, watching her from a distance. She hadn't moved in the past few hours. She had become too weak, and we just stood around, hoping for the best but preparing for the worst.

We checked her in later that day against every last one of her wishes. She tried to push me off, the same way she did when she had enough strength to do it, but it just wasn't there. That hurt me to the core, but I knew it was going to come to this eventually. I sat in the hospital chair next to her bed, flipping through the channels with the remote on the bed. Immediately, I felt the sudden urge to throw up. Uncle Stew looked at me,

"Lyric? You aight?"

"Yeah, I'm going—"

I got up and rushed to the bathroom before I could finish. I threw up into the toilet for a few minutes as I heard knocks on the door,

"Excuse me? Are you all right in there?" It was a female's voice. I figured it was the nurse.

"I'm good. I'm good," I said, as I threw up seconds after that. She opened the door, seeing me seated on the floor hugging the toilet.

"Oh my goodness," she said as she ran towards me, "Do you still need to throw up?"

I shook my head no as she helped me up, back into the room.

"What have you eaten today?"

"No, it's not that. I've been feeling like this the past few days. It only comes at certain times of the day, though. Usually the morning."

She looked at me quizzically. "Do you think you're pregnant?"

"Pregnant?"

I looked towards Big Mama. She was sound asleep.

"No, I am not pregnant!"

She laughed. "I mean, you're at a hospital. Do you want to test just to see if you are? I mean, it would put you at ease and keep you from thinking that there is something else going on with you."

Uncle Stew spoke up, "Gone head and get tested, girl. I already got Mama goin' through this. I don't need something else happening to another one of y'all. Please, Lyric?"

I looked at him and shook my head. "Aight. I'll take the test."

An hour later, I sat in the room, speechless. As many times as I had sex with Junie and didn't get pregnant, I figured that it just wasn't possible. I wasn't prepared for this. Not even in the slightest way.

"Don't be sad, Lyric." Uncle Stew said, "Having a baby is a blessing!"

"I'm not tryin' to hear that right now."

He laughed. "You know what's funny about that? I swear I'm having deja-vu because I remember yo' mama sayin' the same damn thing when she found out she was pregnant with you. It's actually scary now that I think about it."

The nurse came back in with papers about new pregnancies and what to expect each trimester. It took everything in me not to take those papers and throw them back in her face. Just then, my mind went back to Chicago. "The rape," I said louder than I wanted to.

"Rape? Were you raped?" The nurse looked at me.

I looked over at my uncle as he stood up with a concerned look on his face.

"No, no I wasn't raped. I had sex voluntarily. I'm sorry, I was just… I honestly don't know what I was thinking."

The nurse looked at me, unsure if she should believe what I was saying.

"Are you sure?"

"Yeah, I'm good. I'm pregnant, and nobody forced me to have sex."

I picked up the papers, finding something to randomly ask a question about. "So, how long is this morning sickness shit going to last?"

"Well, it generally lasts up to about 14 weeks." She sighed.

"14 weeks? Damn!"

I rubbed my stomach, "Yo' little ass is in there cuttin' up already. 14 weeks?"

"If you ain't yo' mama's child, I don't know who is." Uncle Stew laughed and headed out the door. "I'ma go back in there with Mama."

When he left, the nurse turned to look at me. Her blue eyes were full of compassion. Her blonde hair brushed the top of her shoulders as she reached over and gripped my hand.

"Listen, I've been raped before myself. I know it's a horrific experience but it, unfortunately, it happens because of some sick, sick people. Now, if you want to—"

I cut her off. "I'm fine. I wasn't raped, aight. Damn. I just came in here to see if I was fuckin' pregnant, not to get into no fuckin' counseling session."

The nurse raised her eyebrows and released my hand. She didn't deserve that, but it was just the stress getting to me. The fact that I didn't know whether the baby in my stomach was from Nasir or if it was by the nigga who raped me in Chicago. I was just about four weeks pregnant, so it was anybody's guess as to whose it was. The nurse headed out the room, but I grabbed her attention.

"I'm sorry for blowin' up on you like that. I mean, I just got a lot on my mind right now. It's stressful, you know? My grandma is on the verge of dying, and now I'm about to deal with a pregnancy that I'm not even prepared for, you know?"

She turned around and stood next to the bed.

"I understand it is stressful for you. If you get to the end of this pregnancy, and you still believe that you're not ready, adoption is always an option. You don't have to go through this alone."

"Thank you."

"You're welcome. Now here, take these papers and get back in there with your Grandma. I'm sure she'll be happy to hear the good news."

"If she could, she would whoop me for having a baby out of wedlock. That's how Big Mama is, though. You gotta love her." I laughed.

I walked back into the room. Big Mama was still asleep. She hadn't opened her eyes since she tried to fight me off for bringing her here. The nurses came in to check her vitals from time to time and then left without saying a word to us.

"Unc, I gotta make a run."

"Go head, Lyric. I ain't goin' nowhere."

"Aight. I'll be back later on."

"Ok. I'll text you if anything changes."

I called Nasir and asked him to meet me at Mayfair. It was a mall in one of the city's suburbs, away from all the drama. He was waiting by the entrance when I walked up to him.

"Whassup, baby."

He put his arms around me and squeezed tight.

"Hey, Nas."

"I'm glad you asked me to meet you up here. I got some shit I need to pick up."

I saw him look to his right as somebody waved him down. "Hold on right quick."

He walked over to the passenger's side of a black suburban and handed him something in a swift motion. *Damn, that muthafucka is Junie*, I thought as he walked back to me.

"Aight, let's roll."

We walked through the mall, going in and out of stores and picking up things on the way. He had money, a lot of it, and it showed. He had retro Jordans on his feet with True Religion jeans. Those weren't cheap at all. At least $600 altogether.

"Nas, what the fuck do you do?"

He looked at me. "What you mean?"

"Like, what the fuck do you do? You said you was here on business, but you never went further than that."

"Because I can't."

"Nas."

"What?"

"Come on, now. Look, you tell me a secret, I'll tell you a secret."

"How do I know you got something I want to know?" He laughed.

"Trust me on this."

"Aight. I'm a hustler. Something like a boss."

"Oh, shit. Here we go." I laughed out loud. "Every muthafucka that comes to Milwaukee from out of town swears up and down he was a boss in some former life."

"Aight. If you don't believe me, that's on you. But don't say I never told you."

"What you sell, then?"

"Cocaine."

He pulled out his phone and showed me pictures of bricks he had hidden in his car and other places that the police would be hard-pressed to find.

"God-damn, nigga. Shit!"

"I know."

"What the fuck you come here for with that? This ain't the city."

"Shit, this city is perfect. It's Muthafuckin' crackheads on every block here. I took over Cleveland when I was there then a nigga put me on Milwaukee. So, I came through here and found out it's a nigga named Big Tuck runnin' shit."

"Big Tuck?" I looked at him with wide eyes.

"Yeah. Big Tuck. You know the nigga?"

"I don't know him. I know of him, though."

He looked at me with a raised eyebrow. "Well, what do you know of him?"

Pow! Pow! Pow! Screeeeeeech! The scene of Junie's death flashed in my mind quickly and made me freeze in my path. He tapped me on my shoulder to get my attention.

"Lyric? You aight?"

"I'm good."

We started walking again, and I said, "I just know that he runs shit here, you know what I'm saying? And that nigga doesn't fuck around."

"Word?"

He smiled, "That's cool. I don't fuck around either. I came here to take over this city and if he in the way then… he'll get moved out the way."

He was on a mission. I still wanted to get back at Big Tuck for killing Junie but until now, I didn't have an idea of how to do it. I didn't have a way in, but now, I did. Just then, Junie's Mom popped up in our path. She smiled when she saw me.

"Lyric! Hey, sweetheart!"

She ran and hugged me as Nas watched our interaction.

"Oh my God, how have you been? It's been months! I wish you came around more!"

She looked to the right and saw Nasir. Her mouth hung open as she looked at him in shock like she had just seen a ghost.

"I'm sorry Mrs. Butler, I was just—"

"No, no, baby," she said, still looking at Nas, "it's alright. It's quite alright."

The awkwardness was building until Nas finally said something to her.

"Uh, hello?"

"I'm sorry for staring, sweetie. I really am, it's just. My God, you look like Junie"

"I know, Mrs. Butler. I was thinking the same thing."

Nas responded, "Who is Junie?"

Mrs. Butler looked at me. "I need you to come by my house, ok? I mean, as soon as you can. Please do that for me?"

"Ok Mrs. Butler, I will."

"Thank you, baby."

She kept her eyes on Nas for a few moments as tears fell from her eyes. Suddenly, she turned and walked away.

"What the fuck was that about?" Nas said, looking at Mrs. Butler walk down the mall until she was out of sight.

"I don't even know. I wish I did, though"

Later that evening, I drove to Mrs. Butler's house. She sat in the living room with her husband and a photo album flipped open. She gave me a hug and led me into the front room. She didn't say anything to me. She just opened the photo album and turned to pictures of Junie when he was a baby. There were pictures of him and his sister posing with another boy. The boy was in all the pictures up until Junie turned one. After that, the pictures of him were gone.

"I gave him up for adoption." Mrs. Butler said. "We just didn't have the room for him. It was hard. We couldn't feed all of them, so we did what was best for our boy. We gave him up but that boy you had at the mall with you? I know for a fact that's my boy. When I looked him in his eyes, the connection was there. He looks just like our boy."

She turned to her husband. "He looks just like Junie, baby. He looks just like Junie."

They embraced each other, crying, as I sat in the front room. All along, I felt like he was Junie and I couldn't explain it. From the dimples to the complexion to the personality and all. I almost couldn't believe it. The man I fell in love with is Junie's brother. How the fuck does something like this happen?

I sat in the hospital, fighting back tears as I looked at Big Mama. Tubes ran out of her nose and mouth as she laid there, helpless. I walked over to her bed and held her hand when I saw her eyes open up. The gray life they once had were fading away into the shell that she was becoming. I could tell she used all of her strength to force a smile on her face.

"Hey, baby."

"Hey, Big Mama."

"How are you doing?"

"I'm ok. How are you?"

"Oh, baby, Big Mama is doin' fine, hear?"

I gripped her hand tighter, knowing that she wasn't, but I didn't have the heart to say anything about it.

"How is my great-grandbaby doin'?"

Uncle Stew said he told her I was pregnant when I was gone. I was pissed that he took that away from me, but he said I wouldn't have told her and the more I thought about it, he was right. I didn't want her thinking about another sin I committed while she was on her deathbed. He said that all she did was a smile and say that the baby was going to be just as hard-headed as its Mama.

"The baby is fine, Big Mama. It has me throwin' up all the time, but it's fine."

"Yes, baby."

She coughed a couple times, and I waited for her to catch her breath again.

"That's just the beginning. Wait until the baby actually get out here. You gon' see what it's like to raise a knucklehead."

She smiled again as I laughed. There were peaks of life shining through her sickness and that alone gave me hope that she was going to be alright at some point. Maybe not in this life but definitely in the one to come.

"I guess so, Big Mama. I guess so."

She let the silence sit between us for a few moments as the beeps from the machines in her room kept it from being too quiet.

"Reach over there and grab that bible off the table."

I did as she asked.

"Now, turn to Ro—" She paused to catch her breath. "Romans 8 and 28."

It took me a while to find the scripture. I hadn't turned the pages of a bible since she forced me to go to church with her when I was in high school.

"You got it, baby?"

"Yes, Ma'am."

"Now, read it for me."

"All things work together for the good of those who love the Lord and are called according to his purpose."

"Now, you see. I love the Lord. There is something about suffering that brings the true faith out in people. It causes not only our faith," she paused to catch her breath, "but those around us to have more faith as well. That baby in your stomach has a purpose. You have a purpose. We all do. It's just a matter of going down the right path to get to it. You have to—" She started coughing but this time, it didn't stop.

"Big Mama?" I said, as panic began to take over my body. "Big Mama?"

Moments later, doctors rushed in. They escorted me out of the room as they went to work on her. I wiped tears from my eyes as I paced up and down the hospital hallway. When it became too much for me to bear, I kicked over one of the hall chairs in anger. I didn't understand why this had to happen to her. She said that this would increase the faith of those around her, but all it did was cause me to become bitter towards God—the one that could stop this from happening if He wanted to but yet He did nothing about it. He just sat there and watched the life slowly leave her body. A God like that is not a God I want to know. Eventually, the doctor found me in the hallway, sitting in one of the chairs. I stood up when he approached, expecting the worse. He took a deep breath,

"Ms. Sutton, your grandmother has taken a turn for the worse. Her cancer is progressing quicker than we can stop it. She doesn't have much longer."

I took a deep breath and hung my head. "How much longer?"

He hesitated to tell me, "Maybe a week. If that."

Silence flooded the hallway. I heard footsteps walking behind me, and moments later, a hand was placed on my shoulder.

"Hello, Stewart," the doctor said. "Regrettably, I was just informing your niece about your mother's situation."

"Oh?"

"She only has a few more days. I wouldn't give her more than a week."

His hand gripped my shoulder unconsciously as he stood there with flowers in his hand. I caught them out of the corner of my eye as they began to fall to the ground, seemingly in slow motion. The flower pot he carried them in shattered when it hit the ground. His grip on my shoulder loosened as he began to lose his balance.

"Uncle Stew!"

I reached out to grab him as the doctor helped me. He called for more help as they led him to one of the chairs in the lobby. Someone checked his pulse and turned towards me.

"He just fainted. He's going to be alright."

Moments later, I threw up right next to the shattered flower pot. It was a mess in that hallway. I would've never imagined in a million years that Big Mama would be gone, and there would be nobody else left but me and a sane Uncle Stew. It's funny how things shape up. After they got Uncle Stew back on his feet, we walked into the room. Big Mama was laying in the bed, her cheekbones clearly visible now. Much more than they were before. Her skin hung off of her face like bags as she lay under the covers. I walked over and kissed her on the cheek.

"Uncle Stew, I gotta step out for a minute, ok?" I said.

"Ok, Lyric."

He gave me a tight hug before I left and kissed me on the cheek. It felt right when he did it. I felt the love behind it all, and if there was any bright spot in what was happening to Big Mama, it was that I found another family member to help me through this time.

I headed over to Nas's house. He lived on the east side of Milwaukee on 4th and Burleigh. It was right in the heartbeat of the hood, but I was always over in that area when I was growing up, so it was like a second home to me. I walked up the wooden steps to his house that were on the verge of cracking and causing someone to fall right through. He told me where the strongest parts of the levels were so I wouldn't be the one that fell. When I rang the doorbell, one of the guys he stayed with came to the door with a shotgun leaning on his shoulder. He was tall and stocky. The whites of his eyes were a yellowish color as if he had jaundice. It looked as if he didn't smile a day in his life.

"Whassup Loc, Nas in?"

He opened the door, "Yeah, he in the back. Come on."

He looked around the neighborhood when I walked in as if he was making sure nobody followed me. I had only been here a couple times, but when I did, there were always at least four guys there. Tonight was no different.

"What up, Suzie," one of them said to me as I made my way through the house. I shot the deuces at him and kept walking to the back. Nas sat in his room, counting money and wrapping it up in rubber bands.

He spoke to me before he even looked in my direction. "What good, mama?"

He didn't even lose his count. Mama? I thought to myself. Did he know I was pregnant? Nah, he couldn't know. There was no way. I looked down at my stomach, paranoid as if I was already showing. The pamphlets the doctor gave me told me that it could take up to four months for me to start showing, so I knew it wasn't possible yet. Not in my fourth week. I calmed myself and sat next to him on the bed,

"Whassup, baby?"

"Shit, just countin' this money. How yo' granny doin' and shit?"

I sighed, "She could be better."

"That's fucked up, man. I mean, I know shit like that happens, but it's just fucked up when you see it happen to you or your loved ones."

He wrapped the last bit of money with a rubber band and called Loc to the back room. He came back with the shotgun still in his hand.

"Fam, put that shit up for me." He tossed him a brown paper bag with all the money in it. "That's 54 G's right there, aight."

Loc nodded and left the room with the bag in his hand. Nas got up and shut the door behind him, then got on top of me and kissed me on my neck. I melted in his arms. Immediately, it reminded me of what Junie's mom said to me. I had to know more.

"Baby?"

"Whassup?"

"Do you know who your parents are?"

He stopped kissing me and raised his head up, "What you mean?"

"Do you know who your parents are?"

"Yeah. Eddie and Sheila Macon. Why?"

I looked around the room, hesitating to go further. What if he didn't know he was adopted, I thought to myself. I didn't want to open something up that he wasn't prepared to handle. He sat up on the bed,

"Baby, whassup? Spit that shit out."

"Ok. I mean like, are they your real parents?"

"Lyric, where you going with this?"

"Fuck it; I'm just 'bout to ask you. Are you adopted?"

He leaned his head back and sort of smirked at me,

"Yeah. I am. What even made you ask that, though?"

"You remember that lady at the mall the other day that came up to us?"

"Yeah."

I took a deep breath. "That's your mother."

"How you know it's my mom, Lyric?" He stood up.

"Because, I know her. I used to…." I hesitated, not knowing how he would feel if I told him the truth. Not knowing what he would do. "I used to work for her a little while ago, and she said you were her son. She showed me baby pictures of you and everything."

"That's bullshit, Lyric. Just 'cause a bitch tell you that I'm her fuckin' son don't mean I am." He waved his hands at me in frustration.

"But I'm sayin', Nas, you look just like the other kids in the pictures. I mean, your brother. Y'all, look just alike. I mean exactly alike… and then your sister." I stood up.

His eyes lit up as I spoke like he was trying to come to grasp with what I was saying but his mind just couldn't accept it.

"Nah, fuck that, Lyric. I ain't got no brothers and sisters. I'm an only child, and my fuckin' Mama and Pops is in fuckin' Cleveland right now. They ain't from no got-damn Milwaukee. So just kill this shit, aight?"

Even as he was snapping, yelling, and pacing the room, I saw Junie. I saw his temperament. I had to stop myself from calling him Junie a couple times as he went off. He was doing the same thing Junie would have done. I backed off,

"Aight, Nas, aight. Damn. Just chill, my bad for bringin' the shit up."

He was upset as I walked over to him and grabbed him from behind, putting my hands on his chest. We stood right in front of the mirror while he looked back at me.

"Damn, you got a fat ass."

I laughed. His arms and chest were covered with tattoos all the way down to his wrists. As much as I wanted to stay away from the thug ass niggas, I was drawn to them. It was just something about them that kept me coming back, and Nas had everything I wanted. He was Junie, but just a little meaner. Just a little harder. He was perfect for me, and I wasn't going to let him go. He turned around and put his hands on my ass, bringing me closer to him. I kissed him on his lips, and he spoke right after,

"Yo, we getting' ready to move in on that nigga Big Tuck."

My eyes lit up, "For real?"

"Yeah. Niggas have been keepin' an eye on him for a couple weeks now. Watching how he move and shit. He keeps a tight security watch around him, though; you know what I'm sayin'. It's just a matter of finding a way to break through that shit."

"You sure you want to do this?"

"What you mean am I sure? This is why I came here. I came here to fuckin' run this city and move on to the next. That's it."

"Aight."

He let me go and walked to the window that overlooked the backyard, and I followed right behind him. He had three pit bulls back there tied up to thick ass chains. They wagged their tails when they saw him looking outside at them.

"I just need a plan and shit to get in there. This can't be any fuckin' shootout. I don't want it messy like that. I just want to get in, off that nigga, and then move out. Like a fuckin' ghost and shit, you know what I'm saying?"

The thirst for revenge crept into my blood. It was right in front of me. All I had to do was take it.

"What if I helped?"

He turned to look at me, "Help what?"

"Help you kill that nigga."

He laughed, "I don't know, baby. I mean, I know you rap and shit like that but that ain't gon' help us right now. The fuck you gon' do? Beat him to death with bars you spit or somethin'?"

"Ha, ha, ha. Very funny with yo' lame ass jokes. I'm for real, though. Answer this: What type of nigga would turn down some pussy?"

He stopped laughing.

"Hold up, is this a trick question? I know chicks be tryin' to catch a nigga up and shit."

"Nah, I'm askin' straight up. No bullshittin'. What type of nigga would turn down some pussy? I mean, if you ask me, the quickest way for a nigga's downfall is pussy."

He turned around and sat down on the bed. "I'm listening."

"Aight. Well, let's say I get friendly with one of his chicks and shit, you know? Like some bisexual ass shit. Then, I get it to where you know; he thinks I'm about to have a threesome with him and the chick. As soon as that happens, you sneak in there and kill him."

"You know what, that shit might actually work. Damn. I knew you were a thug ass chick but now, you on a whole 'nother level! Got-damn!" He smiled and nodded his head.

I smiled. I knew he thought I was doing this for him, but this one was for Junie. That boy still had a place in my heart and he would, no matter what.

Pow! Pow! Pow! The gunshots from the night he was murdered rang through my head again as I went into a daze. Nas was talking in the background, but all I heard was noise. I couldn't make out anything he was saying. He grabbed my arm, regaining my attention,

"Lyric? Fuck, you aight?"

"I'm good, why?"

"I was callin' yo' name for like two minutes and shit."

"My bad, Baby, I'm good. Whassup?"

"We need a backup plan, though. Let's say I can't get in there to him."

Pow! Pow! Pow!

"Then I will kill him."

"You'll kill him?"

"Yes. I will fuckin' murder that nigga myself."

"Damn. That shit is gangsta'. For real. That's why you are my bitch, straight up."

I smiled and walked over to him as he sat on his bed. He put his hands on my ass as I leaned him back and climbed on top of him. He pulled a gun out of his waistband and sat it on the bed as I leaned down, kissing him on his chest. It didn't take long for him to pull my pants down and flip me over. He fucked me right in front of the mirror as I arched my back into him, damn near pulling the sheets off the bed as he put his dick deep inside of me. I looked up into the mirror as my mind played tricks on me, flashing Junie's face on him and then morphing back to his own. I licked my lips as he smacked my ass. I didn't care which one of them it was because, to me, they were the same person. I was becoming his bitch, the down ass bitch that would do anything for him. The one that would do anything for Junie and with them both together in one person, there was no limit to what I would do for them. He fucked me harder as my titties bounced back and forth in the mirror. I was home, and this is where I wanted to be.

Chapter 12

I stopped at the house for a while after I left Nas's crib. The silence there was so eerie that I almost turned around and left, but I resisted the urge. I went into big Mama's room and made her bed up the way she always did and cleaned the dust off everything in her room. If she was going to die, I was going to leave her room exactly the way she kept it. Come to think of it; I had no idea how I was going to continue paying for the mortgage when she left. I had no idea what Uncle Stew did for money, but I was sure that it wasn't enough to maintain the house payments. The rapping I was doing here and there brought in a little money, but that wasn't enough either. On top of that, I had a baby coming, and I had no idea what to do with it. I didn't know who the father was, and I wasn't trying to keep a baby that was the product of rape. I couldn't bring myself to do it. It was late when the doorbell rang. I walked to the curtains and pulled it back. Vincent was standing on the other side, patiently waiting for the door to open.

"Whassup, Lyric"

"What good, Vinny?"

We shook hands as he walked in and somberly asked, "How is Big Mama?"

"Shit, she ain't good. Doctors say she got a week and shit." I closed the door behind him.

He shook his head. "Damn, L. Damn. How are you holdin' up?"

"Shit, the best I can I guess."

I walked to the kitchen asking over my shoulder, "You want somethin' to drink?"

"Yeah, I'll take water if you got it."

I walked back out with two bottles of water in my hand, tossing one to him as he sat back on the couch almost timidly. There was something on his mind. I couldn't tell what it was, but I knew it was something that was bothering him.

"The fucks up, nigga? You sittin' there like somebody just ran over your puppy and shit."

"Me and my roommate 'bout to fuckin' get evicted and shit. I ain't got no fuckin' where to go, either."

"Evicted? Y'all ain't payin' y'all rent?"

"Shit, I was. I was givin' my half to him and shit, but it turns out that he was takin' my half of the money and spendin' it on bullshit. Like, the muthafucka would come home with boxes of new shoes and shit, and I'd just be like, damn, this nigga gettin' paid. I need to work on his job and shit, you know? It turns out, the nigga ain't paid rent in three months."

"Damn. That's fucked up, Vinny."

"Ain't it."

"I woulda' beat the shit out that nigga."

"You think I wasn't? When I got to the crib, the letter was on the floor and shit, and most of his shit was gone. I don't know where that nigga went."

"Fuck. Sound like the same shit Quandra did to me."

"Anyways, I'm just like... fuck dude. I don't know what to do."

"How long before you gotta get out?"

"A week. The fuck I'ma do in a week?"

I looked around at the house. I knew with the type of work he did he could support the bills in this house, especially if Uncle

Stew and I chipped in. Big Mama had known him for nearly his whole life, and if she was to trust anybody to live here, it would be him. I mean, it just felt like it was lining up correctly for him to step in.

"You know what, Vinny. Let me see what I can do about you stayin' here for a minute."

"Nah, Lyric. I can't have you bring that shit to Big Mama right now. Not in the state she in now."

"Nigga, shut up. What, you wanna be livin' on the streets and shit? You know it gets cold as hell up here in the wintertime. Yo' nuts will freeze the fuck off. You want that shit to happen?"

He laughed, "Hell Naw, I just—"

"You just gon' shut the fuck up and let me handle this for you, aight? You are my nigga, dude. We been cool for too long to let somethin' like this happen to you and I'm in a position to do something about it, you know what I'm sayin'? So just shut the fuck up and let me work."

He stood up, "Aight Lyric. Man, I just umm…"

"Aye, it's all good, Vinny. It's all good."

He shook my hand and left moments later. I knew what he wanted to say, even if he couldn't get the words out on his own. He was almost like another son to Big Mama. She had a lot of those around here, but I knew that he was special to her. Maybe it was because he replaced Stewart for her the same way Nas is replacing Junie for me. Either way, he was going to live here for a little while. It was for the best.

Big Mama passed away two days later. Me and Uncle Stew were in the hospital when she took her last breath. I remember her turning over to look at both of us as we stood next to her. She smiled and told us that she loved both of us and couldn't wait to see us again. I kissed her on the forehead and Uncle

Stew kissed her on the cheek, and right after that I saw the life leave her body. It was like she took a final gasp of air and that was it. Her eyes closed, and she just laid there, motionless. I had cried so much that by then, it was just time for me to accept the inevitable. We hung our heads and held her hands, taking deep breaths to help us accept what had just happened. The doctors came in soon after and it was official. She passed away at 8:14 pm on July 2nd. A new chapter began.

It seemed like everybody in Milwaukee showed up to her funeral. People I hadn't seen since I was in elementary school came up to me, hugging and kissing me as if I just saw them yesterday. I let it slide, though. It was a real emotional time, and I understood what was going to come with it. Uncle Stew and I sat in the front of the church as the sanctuary filled behind us quickly. Personally, I just wanted the day to be over with. I wanted to put her to rest so I could grieve away from all these people. There was no way I would do it while they were all here. It was something personal to me.

We made our rounds to the front of the church, looking at her one last time before the casket was sealed. She didn't have much makeup on, but she was buried with her pearl necklace and pearl earrings. It was the two things she always made sure she had on when she wanted to be fancy. I smiled as I looked at her in the casket. She was peaceful. No longer in pain, and that alone was enough to send comfort into my heart. I sat down next to Uncle Stew as the pastor began the eulogy. He gripped my hand and tapped my leg as the pastor spoke.

"Today, we are mourning the life of a woman who meant everything to us. We are celebrating the life of a woman who meant everything to a lot of people. To some of us, she was a mother. To others, she was an aunt, a sister, or a friend. She never held her tongue and always told you the truth, no matter if it hurt your feelings, and if you wanted to fight about it, she wouldn't back down from you, either."

The people in the audience all laughed when he said that.

"Yes, she was a strong, strong woman and she will be dearly missed. Let us not forget what this means, though. We all know that this life that we live here is just a test to determine where we spend our next lives. We know that Irma May Sutton is not still in the shell inside this casket. We know that she is somewhere full of joy and happiness. Somewhere far from pain. Far from the craziness that is going on in this city. She is beyond those pearly gates with our savior. The place where, I hope, that all of us want to be some day. Now is not the time to be selfish and follow your own path. We all have a purpose and Miss Sutton surely filled her Godly purpose while she was here on Earth. She did everything God told her to do and changed lives because of it. Now, we can follow our own path and end up in a place that God forbids or we can be obedient and follow his path for us. Is it your choice? Yes. But understand that God loves us so much that he would allow us to go to hell. It's free will. But there is a price or a reward to pay for it all."

It rained hard as we rode to the burial site, and it was fitting for it to be that way. Big Mama loved the rain. She said on the day she gets buried; she wants rain from heaven to fall on all of us. I didn't understand why but I took it as a sign that God heard her and gave her what she wanted. The words the pastor spoke resonated in my heart as I rode in the back of the hearse with Uncle Stew. I thought about the revenge that was buried deep in my heart for Big Tuck. I knew that wasn't God's plan for my life, but then I looked at Big Mama and how she just died of cancer. If that was God's plan for me, then I didn't want that either. The thunder roared in the sky as if it was Big Mama disagreeing with me. I laughed, she always had a way to get to me. Even beyond the grave. Uncle Stew grabbed my hand and squeezed it as we approached the graveyard.

"You ready?"

I nodded my head in agreement as they opened the door for us to get out. He held an umbrella over me as we walked to the site. I saw Shaunie and Vincent standing not too far away from us. I waved for them to come closer to us, but they shook their heads. I guess they just wanted to respect the family and let us have our moment alone. Before I knew it, Uncle Stew walked over and grabbed both of them by the hand and led them over to where we stood. I told Uncle Stew about Vinny. About how he reminded Big Mama of him when he was gone, and it was like immediately after that, Uncle Stew took him in as his little brother. I figured it was his way of thanking Vinny for filling his spot while he was gone and filling that void in Big Mama's life. It was that reason alone that he didn't mind Vinny staying at Big Mama's house with us.

"If he was that close to y'all, then the boy is family. Shaunie, too," he said when I explained everything to him. Lightening lit up the sky as we all stood by the casket, watching them lower Big Mama into the ground. I walked away from them and stood in the rain as they slowly dropped her down to the ground. I couldn't hold my tears in any longer but at least, while I stood in the rain, nobody would know I was crying. Nobody would know the pain that I was feeling right now, and that is all that mattered. A new chapter in my life was about to begin, and only God knew how it was going to end.

Chapter 13

It had been a little over a week since Big Mama's funeral. The grieving period was still thick in the house, but we were maintaining the best we could.

"Got-damn, Lyric. That's the third time you threw up this morning. You good?"

I was bent over the toilet in the bathroom as Vinny watched me from the door. I threw up one more time.

"Fuck. I wish I was. Shit," I answered.

He grabbed a towel and threw it on my back so I could grab it when I was finished.

"What's wrong?"

"I'm pregnant, Vinny." I stood up and leaned over the sink, wiping my mouth with the towel.

"Pregnant? Shit! When this happen?"

"A few weeks ago."

"Word? With that new nigga, you fuckin' with? Nas? The nigga that look like Junie?"

I wiped my mouth again, "Yeah, that's him."

"Damn. That nigga is a fool, though. I heard about him."

"What you hear?"

"That nigga is movin' weight through the city. Like, some heavy shit."

I turned to look at him, "Yeah. That's what I heard, too."

I walked past him as he stood in the doorway. Vinny seemed to fit right into what we had going on at Big Mama's house.

Uncle Stew worked at a soup kitchen downtown for a couple hours a day, and it brought in a little money, but if it wasn't for Vinny, there was no way we could have maintained anything with the house. I was doing shows, so that helped out as well. We were doing good.

Big Mama's room stayed the way it did when I cleaned up her room a few days before she passed away. People that came to visit her in the hospital left flowers and balloons and things like that. We took them and decorated her room with them. When the balloons lost helium, we tacked them to the walls. It was a surreal memorial for her inside her own home. It really was the quietest room in the whole house. I'd fallen asleep on the floor in there a few times, and it felt as if she was right there in the room with me. It was kind of spooky at first, but that only lasted a short time. Right after that, I was calmed by that same feeling.

I walked back into my room just as my phone lit up with a text message from Nas: *Whassup. Yo, I set up a show for you. Hit me up.*

That was the last thing I wanted to hear right now. I just got done throwing up everything I had for breakfast and performing for anybody wasn't on my agenda, but this was for Nas. If it was in my power to do it, I'd do it without a doubt. I called him.

"Whassup baby?"

"Whats good. You sick?"

I coughed, "Nah, I'm straight. Whassup?"

"Aight. Well, I got a show for you to do this Friday. I know yo' Big Moms just passed and shit but are you up for it?"

I wasn't, "Yeah, I'm good for it."

"Aight, bet. I have been keepin' some eyes on Big Tuck's hoes. One of them will be there fa sho. It's at Onyx. I'll point her out to you and shit when we get there."

"Aight, word."

"Cool. Shit, you aight though? Everything good?"

"Everything straight."

"Aight, mama. I'll holla at you later then."

"Aight."

He hung up the phone. I sat on my bed, wondering if I should tell him the truth. I knew that if I said that to him and that baby came out looking nothing like him, it would cause so many problems between us. I didn't want to risk losing him, and I knew that would probably push him over the edge and away from me. I rubbed my stomach as I looked at one of the pamphlets I got from the doctor. I opened the one that was titled, *Your Baby is Growing* and flipped to the 5-week mark.

Congratulations! Your baby is 1/4th the size of your finger! That's right, if you go into your kitchen and take a pea out of one of your cans, you would be looking at a life-size representation of your baby at this moment!

I laughed and tossed the pamphlet down. I couldn't believe that something so small was causing so much drama in my stomach. Laying back on my bed, I started to think about abortion clinics. No, I thought to myself, I couldn't do that. The next best thing to that was adoption, but I couldn't imagine going nine months with a life growing inside of me just to give it away after all the pain. I was stuck between a rock and a hard place as I closed my eyes. I wondered what Big Mama would say to me right now. No, I didn't have to wonder, I knew what she would say.

"Listen here; you're going to have that baby, and you're not giving it away, either. If it was that easy, I'd tell you this, you, yo' mama and yo' uncle would not be here because I would've given both of my children away. There comes a time in life when you just have to face the music. It's not that baby's fault that it's here. Not at all."

She would have threatened me on top of that without a doubt. Even then, I couldn't face the fact that this baby could be the product of rape. I couldn't bring myself to accept that possibility and that alone made me went to get rid of it. I ran my hand across my stomach again as the urge to throw up came back stronger than before. I barely made it to the bathroom.

Chapter 14

Onyx was a night club on Milwaukee's north side. It was large enough to hold concerts, but there were areas of the club that were set aside for regular nights when people just came out to drink and have a good time. I came through the back entry where Nas was standing, waiting for me to show up. He was dressed in all black with a thick gold chain, 80's rap style. He had on dark shades that made him look even more appealing than he usually did to me. He kissed me on the lips when I showed up,

"Whassup, mama? You ready?"

"I'm ready."

The bass from the speakers vibrated the walls as we went down the hallway and into one of the dressing rooms. Loc and a few other men followed right behind us with cold, hard stares, silently warning everyone not to come near us. He sat me down on the chair as the music bumped on the stage.

"Now, you remember what you here for, right? The chick is out there right now. I'ma point her out to you when we get on stage."

"Aight."

"You sure you cool with doing this?"

"Baby, I'm good."

"Cool, cool. We on in a minute. Just chill right here, though, I'ma be right back."

He left the room with two of the men. Loc stayed behind in the room with me; his cold stare never left his grill. My desire to rap was fading as the weeks went by. My focus was shifting to Nas and him only. I fantasized about bein' the bitch right on his side when he went into the drug game. I knew I held Junie back from doing it, but I was more afraid for him. I knew he didn't have the mentality that was needed to get in the drug game like that, but with Nas? I never once thought that he couldn't handle himself. His demeanor said everything that words couldn't say about him and that is what I was drawn to. Outside of the fact that he reminded me of Junie, I knew he could handle himself. Moments later, he walked back into the room and announced,

"Aight, shit. We up."

When we got to the stage, we stood right behind the curtains. Nas pulled me to the side and whispered in my ear the best he could, "There she goes right there. The bitch with the red dress on sitting at the bar."

Around the curtain, I peeked to get a better view. There she was. Thick as hell with a long ass weave in her hair. She looked like somebody who fucked with a drug dealer. Hood as hell, and I saw that just by looking at her.

"You know how to bag her?"

"Shit, I been around bitches like that before. I'm good. I don't need any tips."

He laughed, "Shit, my bad. Aight, do yo' thing then, mama."

He went on stage and seconds later he introduced me to the crowd. Everybody yelled when I showed up on the stage. Even though I was getting tired of the rap game, it was still a surreal moment to hear everybody chanting my name in unison. Nas brought the beat back, and I flowed, the audience was vibing to me with their hands in the air. It was all love. I kept an eye on Big Tuck's chick throughout the set. I had to find a way to see if she was down with fuckin' with a female the way I wanted her to. I told Nas to stop spinning the record.

"Hold up, Nas. For this next song, I need to ask a question to the ladies. How many of y'all are tired of niggas fuckin' with yo' heart?"

Half of the females raised their hands yelling, "Hell yeah!"

"Aight, aight. Now, how many of y'all wouldn't mind tryin' some shit out with another female? I mean, where my freaky ass bitches at?"

The same group raised their hand, and I looked at the back towards the bar where Big Tuck's chick was sitting. She raised her hand to the last question and briefly we made eye contact. It was all I needed.

"You, with the red dress and the fat ass. Come up here!"

It took her a while before she realized I was talking to her.

"Yeah, you! What you lookin' around for? There ain't nobody else in here with a red dress and a fat ass like that. Come up here."

The crowd paused and turned around to look at who I was talking to. She finally got up and made her way to the stage. I thought back to all the females that tried to hit on me when I was stripping in Chicago. I knew what to say to her. Most women loved when another woman was aggressive with them. I took notes and pulled her closer to me when she got on stage.

I whispered into the mic, "So, you gonna' let me taste that kitty?"

She put her hand over her mouth, shocked that I said that on stage. The audience went crazy, urging her to say yes to me. I smiled.

"Come on… I promise I won't bite you… I mean, unless you want it to happen."

I looked over at Nas as he smiled, shaking his head in approval of what I was doing. I cued him to hit the next track. It was a freaky ass song I wrote back in the day for Junie, but I just switched some of the words to tailor it for a female. She ate that shit up like Sunday dinner, and that's all it took. I told her to meet me in the back after the show so we could talk some more before she left the stage. That's all it took for me to get in and set the ball in motion.

After my set, I went backstage to our room. Nas was right behind me,

"Damn, baby. You almost had me jealous up there and shit the way you was grabbin' on her."

"Don't play me, nigga, you know you were gettin' turned on."

He laughed, "Maybe I was, shit."

"I know."

"Yeah, but that shit was dope, though. She comin' back here?"

"Yeah."

"Bet. Well, let me get out yo' way then, you know what I'm saying?"

He stood up and pulled me to my feet, grabbing a handful of my ass while he kissed me. "I'ma leave Man-Man here with you just in case you need him, aight?"

"That's cool."

"Aight. Holla at me later after all the shit gets settled."

"Ok."

He left with three of his guys, and Man-Man stood by the door. Man-Man was short and skinny. He didn't look like the security type, but from what Nas told me, he had a handful of bodies on him. He knew how to kill and get away with it flawlessly. It didn't take long for Big Tuck's chick to make her way to the back area. She came alone with a drink in her hand. Man-Man stepped to the side to let her through. I stood up as she walked towards me seductively. Her lips were just as thick as she was. She came and sat down in front of me, crossing one of her legs over the other, exposing most of her thigh to me. I didn't like women, but for now, I had to play the part. This was not just for Nas; this was for Junie. I put them in my head, and that made it easier for me to go along with the charade.

"So, Miss Suzie Rock. I never knew you were into women."

I sat down next to her, pulling my chair closer. "I'll just say I'm curious, you know? I mean, I'm tired of niggas right now. I figured I might as well see what it's like to be with a woman."

"Oh? So, why me?"

"Look at you. I mean, shit, do I actually need to tell you why? You are fine as fuck. Thick as hell. You seem like you are a freak. Am I wrong? Did I get the wrong bitch?"

She laughed, running her hands through her hair before answering, "No, not at all. I'm definitely the right bitch."

"Aight, good."

"But... there is one thing," she said.

"What's that?"

"I'm kind of talkin' to somebody right now. I mean, it's an open relationship or whatever and by the looks of it," she looked me up and down, "he might not mind if you joined the party."

"Shit, you trying to share me already?"

"No. I mean, that's later. If we even get to that point. I just wanted to put all the cards on the table, you know?" She smiled.

"Yeah, I know. That's cool. Let's just cross that bridge if we get there. For now, I want to get to know you."

I leaned in closer to her, rubbing her breast as I kissed her on her lips. She giggled. "Alright, that's cool. I'll give you my number, and we can go from there."

She gave me her name and number. Keyonna Chambers. I watched her walk out the room before I got up and went to Man-Man. I tapped him on his shoulder, and we both left the club. As we drove back to Nas's house, I thought about how good it would be to kill Big Tuck. Nothing was sweeter than revenge, and I had been waiting for this chance for almost a year. At the same time, there was no way that I could go through with this pregnancy. I couldn't keep up this act with my stomach getting bigger. As we drove through the inner city, we passed a number of abortion clinics that I knew were strategically placed in the hood for population control. I knew it wasn't the best choice, but then again, I didn't really have another option.

We finally pulled up to Nas's crib. Man-Man put his hand across me, keeping me inside the car. "Wait here," he said as he got out, looking up and down the block and around the car before he went to my side and let me out. They took every precaution with me like I was the queen and I appreciated it. I guess it was something Nas told them to do whenever I came around. I looked for him in the house, but he wasn't there. Loc stood in the kitchen and I walked up to him. He didn't say a word, he just opened the back door and led me to the backyard. I followed the pathway to the back where his dogs were. I didn't hear them at all when I walked down the path. Loc took me to the garage where he was. The dogs were tied up nearby as Nas sat in a chair. When I came in, my eyes bucked open in horror. A man was tied up to a chair, completely naked and beaten.

"Close the door, Loc," Nas said as I walked in. He was breathing hard. The dogs were growling. The man was screaming through a gag that was in his mouth. Nas looked over at me.

"See baby; this is what happens to niggas when I come home and find them snoopin' around my shit. I don't ask questions. I just fuck them up until I get tired, and if they still breathing, then we can talk. If not, then fuck it. Lesson learned the hard way."

He turned back towards the man who looked at me in horror. Open wounds and small gashes were all over his body as blood dripped from him like drops of water from a leaky faucet. The dogs growled, lunging for the man but getting yanked back each time. Nas stood up and walked over to him, sliding on brass knuckles. He raised his hand and struck him in the face three times as the man yelped out in pain.

"Bitch ass nigga. I don't know what the fuck he thought this was. Who sent you, muthafucka? Who sent you?" Nas removed his gag and blood dripped from his mouth.

"Nobody! I... I swear to God, nobody!"

"Oh, and you lying in God's name? You're a silly muthafucka."

Nas raised his hand and struck him fiercely three more times, knocking teeth out as more blood spilled from his lips,

"I'm not lying, man, I... I swear I'm not lying! I was just lookin' for..."

Nas grabbed him by the face and snarled, "Lookin' for what, muthafucka!?"

The man started breathing hard, hyperventilating, as Nas continued, "Oh, I know what you was looking for. You were lookin' for death, you bitch ass nigga."

Nas walked away from him, grabbing a knife that was in his chair.

"See baby, this is what happens to fuck boys like this. This is why I'm the fuckin' king. This is why I'm 'bout to run this city. This nigga right here? He is going to be the mouthpiece for everybody that tries to fuck with me or anybody in this set."

He walked back to the man and gagged him again, then began slicing him up with the knife. The man yelled out and tried to break free from his chair, falling over and into his own pool of blood. I covered my mouth and ran out the garage door, throwing up on my way. Minutes later, Nas came out to me. His eyes were filled with a bloodthirsty rage. I didn't even recognize him. For the first time, I felt fear in my heart, and it was at that moment that I knew that this man was truly a boss. Somebody that you couldn't just fuck with and get away with it. I was deathly afraid of what he could do but at the same time, it turned me on and increased my desire to want to be with him.

"Come with me," he said as I heard a single, silenced gunshot come from the garage. Nas kept walking like it was nothing, opening the door for me to walk in first. He took me up to his room, washing his hands in the bathroom as I sat on his bed, completely silenced. He came outside shirtless with a towel in his hand.

"I'm sorry you had to see that, Mama. You caught me in my rage. I never wanted you to see that side of me, but one thing I can't stand is a nigga creepin' in my shit. That's how muthafuckas like me get popped because we ain't watchin'. That nigga thought we were gone but shit, he guessed wrong."

I remained silent as I sat on his bed. Moments later, he came to sit by me. "Baby, did I scare you? I'm sorry if I did."

"Nah. I'm... I'm good."

"You sure?"

"I'm straight. I mean, I ain't never seen any shit like that before, but I'm straight, though."

"Aight then. How that shit go with the bitch from the club?"

I composed myself.

"It went good. Her name is Keyonna. I got her number and shit. We supposed to kick it later on this week."

"Good."

He glanced into the mirror. The bloodthirsty look that was on his face just a while ago was gone. Now, I saw Junie.

"We will be runnin' this city in a minute. And when I say, *we*, I'm talkin' about you and me. My down ass bitch. Every nigga needs one and I know I found mine in you. Right?"

"You know it, baby."

"That's what I like to hear."

Loc and Man-Man dropped me off later that night. The image of that man being tortured in the garage never left my mind. I couldn't bring myself to accept the fact that he deserved it. Either way, I knew what kind of man Nas was, and that wasn't something that he was going to let fly.

The house was quiet when I walked in. I was still too shaken up to go to sleep, so I sat in the front room and turned on the television. I flipped from channel to channel until I landed on a spiritual station. TD Jakes was preaching about the prodigal son. The batteries in the remote died as I tried to flip past the station. I laughed and shook my head, imagining that Big Mama had something to do with that happening. "Nothing is a coincidence, baby," she would say to me when things just seemed to happen at the right time.

"And he came back to his father. That is the issue of the story; he came back to his father, and his father wasn't mad that he left. His father wasn't mad that he went and spent all his money on strippers and alcohol. He wasn't mad at any of that. He was just happy that his son came home after it all. No matter what you have done. No matter what you are doing, you can always come back because your father is waiting for you. His love is still there, waiting for you. His forgiveness is still there, waiting for you. Redemption is still there, waiting for you. All you have to do, child of God, is come home. Just come back and you'll see that the love that you thought was gone is still there, and it is as strong as it has ever been."

I felt a tug in my heart to pray. To ask him for help right then and there but there was resistance. I couldn't go home. This was the same God that took away Big Mama. The same God that didn't save Junie. I didn't want to go back to that God. I didn't want any part of him. I stood up and shut the TV off and just then, I heard a car running right outside my house. Curious about who it was, I walked over to the window, peeking outside. It was past 1 am, so I didn't know who it could have been. I walked to Vinny's room to see if he was there. I cracked the door open, and I was immediately hit with the sounds of his snores. I closed his door and went to the basement, checking for Uncle Stew. He was sound asleep. I went back upstairs, and the car was gone. *I ain't got time for this shit,* I said to myself as I headed back to my room. That's when gunshots rang out. I hit the ground as they pierced through the windows and the door. The barrage of bullets went off for what seemed like forever before the car screeched off.

"Lyric!" Vinny ran out the room, shouting.

Seconds later, Uncle Stew ran up the stairs. "What... what the hell was that?!"

They ran into the front room and saw me laying on the ground, my hands covering my head. Uncle Stew helped me up as Vinny checked out the window.

"It ain't nobody out there," he said, coming back towards us.

"I'ma call the police," Uncle Stew said after he helped me up.

My first thought was to call Nas. I knew he would want blood for what just happened, but I couldn't have him over here with the police. I sat on the couch, breathing slowly, putting together what just happened. Uncle Stew and Vinny were speaking, but I couldn't make out any of the words. It was all going in slow motion, their words jumbled together. My heartbeat seemed to beat loud enough to echo throughout the house. Their words slowly became understandable,

"Lyric, Lyric, you aight? Were you hit? Talk to me?!"

Vinny said as he checked my body for gunshot wounds. Uncle Stew hung up the phone and ran towards me.

"The police are on their way!"

Two squad cars showed up as we all stood on the porch. Some of the neighbors stepped outside their houses, watching from a distance. The officers walked up to us lazily like it was just another shootout in the hood.

The first officer, a tall and slim white man, spoke to us

"So, what happened here?"

I was uninterested in talking to him. "Somebody shot up my house."

"Well, do you know who it was?" He pulled out a pad of paper,

I looked at him incredulously. "No. Do you?"

He dropped the pen and paper to his side. "Listen, Ma'am. We're trying to help you out here."

"How are you helping me by asking me to do your job? It's your job to find out who did the shit, not me."

He began to walk towards me, but Uncle Stew stepped in his path.

"Officer, she is just angry right now. I mean, sir, somebody just shot at her, and they shot up this house. They could've killed all of us, so please, just forgive her for that. Listen, if we knew who did it, we would tell you. But all we can do now is say that our house was shot up."

The other officer spoke. He was a short, round black man with a thin goatee. It looked as if he was the one black officer they sent to the hood to try to sympathize with those who lived there.

"Did any of you get a good look at the car?"

I remained silent, so Uncle Stew answered, "Sorry, officer. I think we were all asleep when it happened."

The other officer spoke up, "Well, how about this. Whenever you guys have an idea about who shot up your home, then give us a call. Until then, don't waste our time."

The officer turned around and walked away as I stood up, ready to walk after him. Uncle Stew grabbed my arm and yanked me backward.

"Don't mind him. He can be a jackass sometimes." The other officer chimed in.

He extended his card to me, but I just watched it sit in his hand. Uncle Stew reached across me and took it from him. "Thank you, officer. I appreciate it."

He tipped his hat and walked away. I didn't see the point of even calling them out there. There was nothing they could do about it, but on top of that, I thought I already knew who was behind it. I remembered Remy threatening me the night I interrupted her on stage. Top that off with me having another show tonight and it wouldn't take a genius to put the two together. Uncle Stew tried to get me to come in the house, but I stayed on the porch. He was scared they were going to come back and finish me off, but at that point, I didn't care. I was going to sit there and wait for them. Vinny took a spot next to me on the porch.

We stayed out there for hours just chilling, not saying anything to each other. The crickets chirped in the distance. The moon glowed brightly above us and the stars twinkled back and forth with each other like they were having the battle to see who could outshine the other. I imagined that it was Big Mama's spirit inside one of the stars. She was always watching over me, and I knew it.

Vinny scooted closer to me. "You know what I love about you?" he asked, looking up at the stars. "You are fearless. You always have been. Even when we were little kids, it was always you that went first. Remember that time our ball rolled up on Miss Vanderson's grass and we were all scared to get it? Then you were like, 'man, forget her' and walked up on her grass while she was standing right there and then threw up yo' middle finger at her. That shit was too funny."

I laughed, "Hell yeah, I remember that. She cussed me out, too, and Big Mama beat the breaks off me. But then she went over there to that witch house and told her if she ever cussed me out like that again that she was gonna beat her worse than she beat me."

He laughed louder, "Hell yeah! Big Mama was a G, on everything. I know where you get it from now. But aye, I'ma get in here so I can get at least a few hours of sleep. You coming?"

I took one last look at the moon's glow.

"Yeah, let's go."

Chapter 15

I sat in the lobby, watching women walk in and out of the offices. Somber, remorseful faces decorated the room like blue Christmas ornaments. I heard baby cries behind me, but when I spun around, there was nothing there but the same women I saw before. *What the fuck?* I said to myself as I turned back around in my chair.

I could hear the faint chants of protesters just outside the door of the clinic. I walked through a swarm of them when I came in. They were holding up signs and trying to hand me pamphlets as I maneuvered through them and into the office. They did their best to detour me, but I was sure this is what I wanted to do. There was no way I could go through these next months pregnant if I was going to keep rapping and being by Nas's side. Especially with the plan to set up Big Tuck. He wasn't fucking with any pregnant woman, and that was just common sense. I just didn't want to take the chance and go through the aftershock of what something like that would bring into my life.

"Sherita Thomas?" a short, white woman said as she came out the back office. Sherita stood up and headed to the front. There was a baby bump that was just becoming visible beneath her shirt. She rubbed her hand over her stomach as she walked to the front, her boyfriend right behind her as if he was prodding her to go forward. I did my best to block Big Mama out of my mind. I knew she would be sending every signal she could to get my attention, but my mind was set. This was something I had to do. The chatter of the protesters outside went lower and lower as time passed by. The baby cries started up again. This time, it felt as if the baby was right by me. I looked to my left and right in a sudden movement, startling one of the women by me. She wrinkled her eyebrows and curled her top lip at me.

"My bad," I said to her as she moved a few seats further down. The short, white woman came out the room again, "Maria Chambers?" She took a deep breath and walked to the front of the room as if she was walking her own green mile. *This is for the best,* I told myself as I sat in my chair. It wasn't long before the white woman called me back to the room.

I followed her down a short maze of hallways, turning to the left a few times and then to the right. We ended in a small room with one table and two chairs. She held her hand out for me to sit down. "So, Miss..." she looked down at her paper,

"Lyric Sutton. I understand that you are about a month and a half into your pregnancy?"

"Yes, that's correct."

She flipped through a few more pages. "Ok. And you're sure you want to go through with this?"

I looked to the right, hesitating for a moment before I responded.

"Yes, I'm sure."

A sharp pain shot through my side when I gave that answer. The pain caused me to squirm in my chair, and the woman reached out to me, "Are you ok?"

"Yeah. Yeah, I'm good. I just felt a pain in my side. I'm good, though."

She looked at me with concern. "Ok, if you're alright, then I will continue. Have you ever had an abortion before?"

"No. This is my first one."

"OK. And are you familiar with the procedure?"

"No, not really."

She went into the step by step process as the pains radiated through my side when she spoke. I held it in, careful not to alarm her because I just wanted to go through with the process. The way she described it all was hard to handle. As she spoke, I began to see visions of a baby boy being held in my arms, looking up at me. He had short, curly hair. It seemed like he couldn't have been any more than five months but he was spoiled. Everything he had on was Jordan brand, and he looked just like Nas. Exactly like him. It was weird thinking that my son would have been Junie's nephew. Either way, I felt like I would have had a piece of Junie inside my son and that's what mattered.

But what if it's not Nas's baby? I thought to myself. The pain shot through my side again, causing me to shut my eyes tight. The lady kept talking as if nothing was happening. The baby cries came back, but now, they were deafening. The woman's words were drowned out, and I finally yelled out when it became too much to bear.

"Wait!"

She jumped backward in her chair, looking at me like I was some sort of anomaly.

"I... I'm sorry, but I don't need to be here. I shouldn't have come in the first place."

I stood up and walked out the room.

"Uh, Miss... Miss Sutton?" she called to me.

Her words fell on deaf ears as I walked back through the labyrinth and made my way out into the lobby. I felt the pain of some of the women there, the confusion. The encouragement from fuck boys that wanted nothing more than to get rid of their responsibilities. I walked out of the lobby with my head high as I heard the same white woman call the next victim in.

Somewhere, I knew Big Mama was smiling down at me. I could only hope that I made the right decision.

I called Nas and asked him to meet me downtown at the lakefront. The same spot where we met the very first time we kicked it. He was a little hesitant about being out in the open like that now since he was moving up in the game but he still came out. Man-Man stood outside his truck like a secret service agent as Nas walked over to me while I sat on the bench.

He kissed me on the cheek. "What good, Mama?"

"Shit. I'm just chillin'."

"I hear you."

He looked out onto the water as the waves moved across the lake.

"I'ma kick it with that chick tonight."

"Word," he said, his eyes still fixed on the water, "What yall gon' do?"

"Shit, I don't know yet. Might just take her to a club or somethin'."

"Nah, Nah. I don't like that shit."

"Why not?"

"Cuz ain't no tellin' if that nigga is gon' be there or some of his guys. Take her to a low-key spot, you know? Somewhere that niggas don't show up."

"Aight. I know a place."

"Cool," he put his eyes on me, "You aight, ma? You look sick and shit."

"Nah, I'm good. My stomach was a little fucked up earlier, but I'm straight."

"Oh?" he said as he ran his hand across my stomach, "Fuck around and be pregnant in this bitch."

My heart skipped a beat, "Pregnant? Nah, I can't be."

"Shit, I know I am fuckin' busted in yo' ass more than once, shit. I know it's possible. I always wanted a son, though, straight up. Somebody to carry on my name just in case I don't make it out this bitch, feel me? Shit. That's all a nigga can actually hold onto now."

"I feel you."

He turned to look at Man-Man. He remained by the car in the same position, his hand near his waist as he surveyed the scene. After a few moments, he turned back towards me.

"I heard about that shit last night."

"What shit?"

"Come on, now. Don't act like yo' shit didn't get shot the fuck up last night."

"Oh… yeah, that ain't shit."

"Fuck that. Who did it?"

"I think it was Remy's petty ass. She had some shit to say to me that night I met you on stage, remember?"

"Remy, huh?"

The look in his eyes resembled the same look he had when he was beating the shit out of that man in his garage the other day. It was a look that I would begin to know and recognize when the killer in him was ready to come out,

"Fuckin' Remy," he leaned back on the bench, "I spray bitches/I don't play with bitches/fuck with me, and I will erase these bitches."

He quoted one of the lines from her songs word for word as he laughed to himself, rubbing his hands together. I knew what he was thinking of doing, and I didn't care to stop him.

Later on that evening, I met up with Keyonna. She met me at Oliver's, a fancy restaurant in a suburb of Milwaukee. A place where the police showed up seconds after you put the call in. I usually smoked or got drunk before I fucked with females to get my mind off the fact that I wasn't a lesbian, but I was hard pressed to do it with the baby in my stomach. I had to do my best to make it believable.

I waited in my car until she texted me: *I'm here. Where you at?*

I got out the car; my skirt went to the top of my knees, and it fit perfectly around my ass. She had on jeans and a low cut shirt, pushing her titties out just enough to lure anyone in. We walked into the restaurant as the hostess peered at us like we didn't belong.

"Can I help you two?" she asked, her voice just a prissy as she looked.

"Two seats, please. Preferably a booth."

She smiled at us generically before leading the way to one of the booths by the window. We walked past various white couples with a few black faces scattered around the room. I didn't mind the attention. It felt as if I was back on stage. The hostess handed us our menus and abruptly walked away from our table.

Keyonna noticed. "The fuck is wrong with that bitch?"

"Fuck her. We here doin' us, and that's all that matter," I said as I scooted closer to her, "So, tell me about yourself."

She smiled, "What do you want to know?"

"What do you do when you not at the club and shit?"

"I work at the crib with my nigga."

"Word," I had a feeling she was talking about Tuck, "Yo' nigga, huh? Doing what?"

"Shit. Countin' money. Makin' sure the house stay in line, you know, that kinda shit. Nothing major."

"Fuck. Yo' nigga must be a fuckin baller then and shit."

"He does his thang. He definitely does his thang."

The pale waiter that came to our table had fixed his glasses before he spoke to us, "Can I get you people any drinks?"

"You people?" Keyonna said, "The fuck you mean you people?"

The waiter's face immediately turned beet red. "No, I didn't mean you people like that. I meant, you people like... you know, you folks? That's all."

She burst out laughing as she watched him stutter through his response. "I'm fuckin' with you, Opie. Let me have a Hennessy and coke," she said.

She looked over at me, "Matter of fact, let's get two."

"Nah, I'm good, Key."

"Fuck that, we getting drunk tonight! I'm tryin' to take advantage of somebody a little later, and it's much more fun when we are both into it."

The waiter quickly turned around and went to prepare our drinks. As we talked throughout the night, I found out more about Tuck than I thought I would. He has a weakness for women with my complexion. Keyonna told me how she gets jealous when he fucks another chick in the threesome better than he fucks her. She said she tried not to let it get to her too much because she knew how crazy he was and the smallest things would set him off.

"You think he would fuck with me?" I asked as I sipped on the drinks the waiter brought back.

She ran her hand across mine, "Well, I'ma test some shit out first and then we'll see about that later."

She ordered a few more drinks for herself and by the time the food came, she was lit. The customers that sat around us shot annoyed looks our way because of how loud she had gotten.

"Shiiit, bitch, I'm tryin' to tell you right now, you are fine as fuck! Oh my, God, I can't wait to put my tongue in that pussy!" It wasn't long before the waiter came back to our table, threatening to call the police if we didn't leave.

"There are complaints from the other customers," he said to us nervously. I brought her out to my car and drove us to a secluded park on the north side of the city. Nobody ever came there, especially at this time of night. It's the park me and Junie used to go to when we were in high school and wanted to fuck. We both lived at home, so it was hard to find a place to get away to, but we eventually came here. It sort of felt like I was desecrating our spot by bringing her here but then again, the connection I made between Nas and Junie was so intense that I began to think that it was him leading me to do it. I pulled into the parking spot right in front of a group of trees. Keyonna looked around.

"Where the fuck did you take me?" she asked.

"Sssssssh."

I let my seat back and pulled her on top of me as she began kissing me on my neck and stroking my hair. As many times as I had been around women, this was the first time I was actually fucking one. She ran her hand down my titties, then climbed between the seats and got in the back. She reached into her purse, pulling out a dildo that was at least nine inches long. She put it all the way in her mouth and pulled it out as she signaled with her finger for me to come back there with her. I climbed towards the back as she put the dildo in my mouth. I gagged when it went halfway in as she laughed,

"Bitch, you gotta' know how to take the dick. There ain't no fuckin' gaggin' allowed!"

She took it and put it all the way in her mouth again while I pushed her back onto the seat, unbuckling her pants. I ran my tongue over her pussy slowly, licking and sucking along the way. She put the dildo back in her mouth to muffle her moans. Her wetness covered my lips as I put my tongue into her pussy. She took my head and pushed it in deeper, throwing her legs over my shoulders. I reached my hand down and played with my own pussy, getting myself wetter in the process.

She stopped me. "No, bitch. I'm about to fuck the shit out of you." She got up and turned me around, strapping on her dildo and pushing it deep inside of me. She smacked my ass like a nigga as she fucked me hard, fast. She pushed it in as deep as it could go while I begged her to keep going. It felt good to me, and it was at that moment that I could see why bitches fucked with other bitches. She flipped me over and snatched the dildo off of her, putting it in my mouth. I licked it, tasting the juices from my own pussy as she shoved it into my mouth slowly, going in further and further until I couldn't take it anymore.

"Yes, bitch, that's how you take the dick. That's how you take the dick." She left it in my mouth as she went down on me, licking my pussy up and down like nobody ever had before. She twirled my clit around in her mouth, sending my eyes back to my head as I sucked on the dildo.

"Ummm-hmmm," she said, "don't that feel good? A nigga ain't gonna make you feel this good." She kept going until I came all over her mouth. She licked her lips, getting it all off as she came and kissed me on the lips. I didn't stop her. "Now, fuck me," she said, bending over, "Fuck me hard, bitch." I figured out how to strap it on, and I fucked her. I fucked her the way Junie and Nas fucked me when I saw them in the mirror. Going in deep and stopping for a few seconds, then going in deep again.

"Smack my ass," she said as I pulled my hand up and dropped it on her ass. The windows have been fully fogged up as we went on for what seemed like hours. She came, slapping her hand on the window like she was trying to get out. She damn near shattered the glass as she pounded it with her fist. Honestly, I think this bitch may have just turned me out. She fucked the shit out of me that night.

I dropped her back off at her car. She had somewhat sobered up by the time we got to the restaurant.

"So, am I going to see you again?" she asked.

"Yeah, you will. Most definitely."

She smiled, "Aight then, bae."

She walked to her car, her ass bouncing with each step she took. I was going to work her until I was able to get closer to Tuck and I was going to have fun doing it. On the way home, I called Nas and let him know what happened. He wasn't even mad that I fucked her. He said if it was a nigga, then he would fuck both of us up, but he didn't feel threatened by a chick. It's probably because if it ever came up, he wouldn't do anything but join in with us, and honestly, the way Keyonna fucked me, it might be a possibility.

"Aye, don't forget the reason you doin' this shit. We need to get to Tuck," he said, reminding me of what was at stake.

"I know baby, I know. That nigga is gonna get his. I'ma make sure of it."

"Aight. Let me know when you get to the crib. I love you."

"Love you, too."

When I got home, I sent two texts. One to Nas and the other to Keyonna. This was turning into a love triangle that I never anticipated.

Chapter 16

I woke up the next morning smelling the aroma of fried bacon creeping into my room. I was surprised when I got out of bed and didn't have the feeling to throw up that I usually had each morning. Maybe I was past that stage, and I was happy about it. I glanced at myself in the mirror and as of now, I still wasn't showing any signs of being pregnant. I could only hope to keep that up for a few more months or at least until I was done with this Big Tuck shit. I walked into the kitchen while Uncle Stew leaned over the stove, frying bacon and scrambling eggs the same way Big Mama did it.

"Whassup, Unc?"

"Little Miss Lyric, just in time for breakfast." He slid a plate right in front of me at the table. "How is my little niece or nephew doing?" he asked as he walked back over to the stove.

"Good. I'm finally not throwing up, so I guess it's getting better."

"Man, I heard you hurling from all the way downstairs a few days ago. I thought you were about to up-chuck one of your lungs into the toilet."

"It felt like it, Unc."

I looked at the wall, noticing the bullet holes that spread out along the top. It was only two of them, and you probably wouldn't even see it if nobody told you they were there. Uncle Stew turned to see why I became so quiet then he followed my eyes up to the bullet holes,

"Oh, don't worry about those, Lyric. I know somebody that will take care of all those for us."

"Who?"

"It's a guy down at the soup kitchen. He's good with that kind of stuff."

I glared at him, "Unc, come on now. Don't be havin' any crackheads up in Big Mama house."

"Lyric, don't be like that," he said, filling his plate with eggs, bacon and grits as he came and took a seat by me, "It's a struggle just like anybody else. Just like mine used to be. We have to help people get through that, not shun them away."

"I hear you, but I just don't want that nigga coming in here and trying to sell Big Mama's stuff like you used to."

"Oh, you don't have to worry about that. That won't be happening, trust me. I checked him on it well before I told him he could come and I'ma have my eyes on him every step of the way. Trust your old uncle this time."

I smiled at him while I enjoyed the breakfast that he made. He made a big turnaround from the days he used to get high and lose himself in his addiction. I was happy to see him like this now and even though I didn't believe him at first, it was going on two months, and he proved me wrong.

"Where is Vinny?"

"I don't know. He was gone when I woke up this morning."

"That's weird. It's Saturday, so I know he doesn't have to work."

"Ain't no telling."

I finished my breakfast and walked into Big Mama's room as Unc stayed behind and straightened up the kitchen. It seemed like when Big Mama left, I started going further and further off into the deep end. I was doing things I'd never done before and to think that I even went to that abortion clinic in the first place was enough to tell me that I wasn't the same person. I had even stopped rapping. I hadn't had a show since the time I met Keyonna, and the only reason I had it in the first place was to meet her.

I went to a picture of Big Mama that sat on the dresser. She was young, at least in her early 30's. Her gray eyes and long, black hair were something most women could only dream of having. Next to that picture was one of my mother. I wished that I was able to get to know her better. The only picture Big Mama had of her was this one on the dresser. She looked into the camera as if she wasn't expecting it to be there; a cigarette hung out her mouth while she had rollers in her hair. Her breasts hung down low under her shirt. I could tell she didn't have a bra on. She looked like one of those women who had the potential to be beautiful, but they just didn't know it yet.

"Yeah, I come in here sometimes myself and just stare at things. It still feels like she's here, you know? I really can't explain it," Uncle Stew said with a smile as he walked into the room.

"Yeah, I see what you mean. It's crazy because… it just doesn't feel like she's actually gone."

He walked over and put his hand on my shoulder. "I know the feeling, Lyric. I know the feeling."

"What do you think Mama would have been like if she never OD'd?"

"Yo' Mama?" he said, laughing with a broad smile that showed three of his missing teeth towards the back of his mouth, "Yo' mama was a trip!" He sat down on Big Mama's bed.

"Honestly, if she was healed from her sickness, I think yo' mama could have been very successful. I could see her being a manager of a bank or something like that. Maybe a teacher.

I mean, she had a way with words and she was real good with money before her sickness. I know that whatever she would have done, she would've made a difference."

He stopped and looked at her picture then turned to look at me. "Lyric, you got everything you need to be successful. Whatever you do, don't let these streets consume you. I know you're out there doing your thing, and I would be one of the biggest hypocrites on this side of the moon if I told you not to. But, just be careful. The saddest thing in the world would be to see you die with all the potential in the world like your mother did. It would be a shame. A complete disgrace."

Just then, the front door opened and slammed shut. I heard footsteps running through the house, and the tennis shoes squeaked to a stop right at Big Mama's door. We told Vinny he could come in the room, but he just felt that he shouldn't, out of respect for me and Uncle Stew. To him, it was like sacred ground. I didn't understand it, but I appreciated him for having that type of reverence for Big Mama.

"Yo, L, I need to holla at you about something real quick."

"What's wrong with you?"

"Yo, just come real quick, aight?"

I followed him out to the porch as he stood, trying to catch his breath.

"Vinny, what the fuck is up, nigga?"

"Aight. Shit. I was over at, um, at Lincoln hoopin' and shit. Remy was up there with some niggas just fuckin' around and shit. It was cool, you know what I'm sayin', just a real cool time and—"

I smacked him on the arm. "Vinny! Quit fuckin' painting the picture and spit the shit out!"

"My bad, aight, but yo, so we were hoopin', and I saw Remy sitting by the car and shit. Then all of a sudden, this nigga comes up to her car and starts talking to her. Like, it seems like he was tryin' to holla at her, but you know, Remy's nigga was right there. So that nigga steps to him, then all of a sudden, the nigga that came up to her pulls out a pistol and just empties the clip on her at point blank range. I mean, that nigga just didn't give a fuck. He just unloaded. Then he pulled out another pistol and started shootin' at the niggas that were with her."

"On what?"

"On everything. Man, I ran out that muthafucka so fast! You didn't hear the gunshots?"

"Nah, I ain't heard shit. I was in there with Uncle Stew."

"Damn. I ain't never seen any shit like that in my life. I fuckin' saw her get murdered. Like, her shit was just exploded as soon as he fired on her. The nigga wasn't even wearing a mask, and the shit was in broad daylight, L. Broad fuckin' day! Niggas is not givin' any fucks in the Mil no more. I gotta get the fuck out of here."

As he rambled on, I thought about Nas. I knew he had something to do with it. There was no such thing as a coincidence, as Big Mama used to say. I knew I was dealing with a killer now and oddly, it turned me on to know that. It made me want him even more. I heard Big Mama's warning, but I pushed it to the side, drowning her out with my own desires.

"Yo, you think yo' boy had something to do with that shit?"

He got my attention. "Who? Nas?"

"Yeah. I heard some shit about that nigga from before. I heard that muthafucka don't be playin' and shit. And the word is, he comin' for Tuck ass."

"Nah, Vinny, you can't believe everything you hear. Nas ain't about that shit."

"Yeah, well that ain't what it seem like. Shit. I'ma just keep my ass in the fuckin' house and only come out to go to work. Fuck hoopin'. Fuck the club. Shit, fuck this porch. I'm goin' in the house right fuckin' now."

He got up and left me outside as I sat on the steps. I pulled out my phone just as I got a text message. It was Nas: *I told you I would take care of it. We will own this city in a minute. Trust. I love you.*

I heard sirens rushing down the streets in the direction of the Lincoln basketball courts that Vinny just left. In the midst of the sirens, children still ran up and down the streets, chasing each other like there was no tomorrow. The cars still sped down the neighborhood streets like there weren't any children around. Everything was going along like there wasn't just a fucking murder just blocks away from here. But this was Milwaukee, though. The violent shit that happened here became so routine that people just expected it to happen, and when it did, they kept on with their lives with no interruption.

Sadly, since Nas came into the city, I knew there would be much more murders before everything slowed down. He said he came here for a reason, and that fire in his eyes was not going to let him settle for anything else, and no matter what, I was going to be right there with him to see it through.

Chapter 17

It didn't take long for Keyonna to open up to me. It had only been a couple of weeks when she told me she wanted to start bringing me around Tuck. She said that she told him a lot of good things about me and that I wouldn't mind being the third wheel in their threesomes.

Nas was ready for it to happen. "You betta not let that nigga fuck you, Lyric. I swear to God," he would say whenever we spoke about what was going to happen. I had no intentions of letting him inside me. None whatsoever. My only focus was revenge. I wanted him to feel pain like the man Nas had in his garage. It was all for Junie.

I still wasn't showing in my pregnancy. I was just about two months in, but from what the pamphlets said, I was right on schedule, so I didn't worry too much about it. I carried one of them in my purse to read when I had the time. The fact that I wasn't showing was even better for what I was about to do. I walked into the front room and flipped the television on. The news about Remy's death was on the news.

"And right here, in broad daylight, Jennifer Marie West was gunned down at Lincoln Park on the city's north side. Known to many as Remy, she was a favorite rapper among her peers. She was shot multiple times and was believed to have died immediately. She was murdered in front of a crowd of people, but even with that, there are no leads or anything about the killer. The police are questioning everyone believed to be there at the time, but they are urging anyone with any information about the shooter to contact the Milwaukee Police Department. This is just another tragic death in the city of Milwaukee."

Nas sent me a text a few minutes later: *Yo, come by the crib.*

I replied: *Ok*

When I got there, a crowd of guys was standing outside of his house. They all had on black like they were about to murder somebody. Loc walked to my car as soon as I got out, escorting me up the steps. They all had cold, hard stares as I walked past them. A few of them gave me a head nod as I entered the house. In just a few weeks, Nas had his spot set up like it was something out of New Jack City. In the room just beyond the front, there were naked women with masks on bagging dope. I peeked in as I walked past, but Los quickly closed the door before I could get a good view of everything. Around the corner, two men sat in chairs with double-barreled shotguns. They had black bandanas tied around their mouths with their fingers on the trigger. We walked past them, and they didn't move their position. We made our way up the stairs and into Nas's room. He stood by the dresser with his shirt off, slicing bricks of cocaine open and tasting them for validity. Loc closed the door as I walked in and said,

"Hey, baby."

"Whassup, mama."

"What you need?"

"I need you to move in on Tuck. You ready for it?"

"I mean… the chick is ready to let me in, you know what I'm sayin', but I don't want to rush shit. She might think somethin' is up."

He walked to the window that overlooked the backyard. The dogs barked as soon as he put his head by the window.

"That muthafucka just robbed one of our spots. Took a little cash and some of the dope. I'm ready to move on that nigga right now; you know what I'm sayin', just show up and shoot his shit up."

I tossed my purse on the bed and walked over to him, rubbing my hand on his back. I didn't really notice the tattoos that covered his shoulder blades until now. Angel wings with words written in the middle, *in God's hands*. I felt Big Mama trying to creep into my thoughts, but I began speaking, doing my best to drown her out,

"Nah, baby. You're smarter than that. That's why you sent me in there. He is expecting you to come in hard like that. He probably is waiting for you to do it, you know what I'm sayin'? This is chess, not fucking checkers. Just use some patience and shit. Let yo' bitch handle it. You can trust me."

"You see, that's why I'm with you. You know how to calm a nigga down and put my thoughts where they need to be." He turned around and kissed me on my lips. The anger in his eyes subsided while he glanced over at the bed.

"The fuck is that?"

He said, letting me go and going over to the bed. I watched him as he grabbed the pamphlet that fell out of my purse. I rushed to take it out his hand, but he moved before I could put my hands on it.

He read the title of the booklet, then looked towards me. "So, you're pregnant?" Why the fuck you got this shit?"

I hung my head low and sat on the bed.

"Lyric," he sat next to me, "Why the fuck you got this?"

"Baby…" I hesitated, "I'm pregnant."

He looked back at the pamphlet, "Pregnant?"

Silence flooded the room as he flipped through the pages of the book. I felt sick to my stomach, knowing that I wasn't sure if he was the father. I felt like he wouldn't believe the rape story but even with that, I wouldn't tell him about it anyway. I was still in the process of blocking it out of my memory, but I was finding that to be nearly impossible. Especially if this baby was a product of that. I was nervous about his reaction even though he told me he wanted to have a son a little while ago. His facial expression didn't change as he flipped from page to page. The seconds felt like it took hours to pass.

"So, we havin' a fuckin' baby, huh?"

He tossed the book on the bed and smiled, reaching for my stomach and rubbing his tattooed hand across the surface. He softened up, lifting my shirt as he bent down to kiss my stomach. It felt good to me and honestly, I felt that we were already a family. I put my hand on him as he went back and forth across my stomach.

"Yeah, we havin' a baby."

"How far along are you?"

"I'm about two months."

He laughed, "Damn! Two fuckin' months? You kept that shit from me for two months?"

"No... I just found out myself because I kept throwing up and shit, so I went to the doctor."

"Word?"

"Yeah. They told me that and then gave me one of these books so I could understand the pregnancy better."

"Aight, cool. Cool."

He smiled again, looking to the side as if he was envisioning a future with his child,

"So I guess we really need to get movin' on this shit with Tuck then. I'm guessing yo' ass ain't got long before you start lookin' pregnant and shit."

"Yeah."

He leaned over and kissed me and it quickly turned into something else. Whenever we had sex, we fucked. It was hard and rough, and I loved that shit, but this time it wasn't like that. This time, his kisses were slower. His movements were melodic like he was moving to some kind of smooth jazz that was playing inside his mind. He stroked my hair and bit my bottom lip softly, caressing every part of my body with his hands. I gripped his tattooed arms, digging my nails into him the deeper he went inside of me, spreading my legs apart as far as they would go. I opened my mouth, wanting to scream out in pleasure but the words didn't leave my mouth. No sounds were made as we laid together, silently fucking each other with tightly-packed passion releasing from our souls. I was in love with him, and there was nothing that could stand between us.

Chapter 18

The next day, I met up with Keyonna at George Webbs, a small restaurant that served breakfast at any time of the day. It was around 5 pm when she walked into the restaurant.

"Hey boo," she said, taking a seat across from me.

I kissed her on the lips, "Whassup bae?"

"Shit. Ain't nothing new going on. I have been thinkin' about you and shit, though."

"For real?"

"Hell yeah. Shit. Damn near got Tuck jealous that I get all googly eyed when I talk to him about you."

"Ain't no need for him to get jealous, I got some shit for him, too."

"I bet you do." She smiled seductively. "But anyways, he tryin' get up with you."

"When?"

"He said, later on, tonight or tomorrow. He gotta handle some business first, but he said he would let me know."

"Aight, that's cool."

The chimes on top of the door rattled when she walked in. It felt like I saw a ghost as I tried to focus my vision. It was really her. I couldn't believe she showed her face in this city again and after the shit she pulled with me in Chicago. Keyonna turned around, following the path my eyes made as it led her to Quandra. She didn't even look to our side of the restaurant as she and a few females she was with walked to a table clear across the room. Keyonna turned back to me; her eyebrows scrunched up together in confusion.

"Who the fuck is that?"

I didn't answer her as thoughts of that night flooded back to my memory. In flashes, I saw the hotel room in a complete disaster; my things were thrown all across the floor, my mattress hung off the frame, and the drawers were pulled completely out of the dresser. I remember the horror that went through my bones when I frantically searched under the bed for the money I kept hidden there just to find it gone. Not only that but every one of Quandra's things were gone too. I remembered that feeling as rage boiled inside my blood. Keyonna moved her lips, but I didn't hear anything coming from her mouth.

When Quandra took her seat, I got up and headed in her direction. They were all talking to each other as one of her friends looked in my direction when I stood behind Quandra.

"Who the fuck is this?" she said as Quandra turned around. Her eyes bucked open as she scooted back in her seat and stood up.

"Oh my God, Lyric!"

She reached out to hug me, but I pushed her arms away from me even quicker. She had a look of misunderstanding on her face.

"What? What's wrong, Lyric? Where have you been? I've been lookin' for you ever since you left Chicago."

"Bullshit."

"No, it ain't bullshit. I swear to God, when I got back to the hotel, I saw all the shit gone. The covers were everywhere, the beds, the dressers were fucked up. I called the hotel front desk, and then they called the police. They thought you were kidnapped and shit, I swear to God, Lyric."

Her friends looked at me quizzically, as if they were waiting for me to react to the bullshit she was feeding me.

"You was lookin' for me?"

"Hell yeah. I mean, I even went to yo' Big Mama house a few times since I came back from Chicago."

Mentioning Big Mama was crossing a line that should have never been crossed. I was seconds away from picking up one of the knives off the table and pushing it through her neck.

"When the fuck did you go to Big Mama's house?"

"I umm… I came back about a month ago, and as soon as I came back, I went to her house to ask about you."

"A month ago?"

"Yeah"

"What did she say?"

"She just told me you weren't home, so when I—"

I swung my fist and hit her in her mouth, knocking her back into one of her friends,

"Bitch! Big Mama has been dead for over a month! She has been in the hospital longer than that! The fuck you come in here lying on my fuckin' dead grandma for, huh!? Bitch!"

I reached over and grabbed her, slinging her into another table as her friends got up. Seconds later, Keyonna came from behind me, knocking one of the girls out with a punch to her jaw. The other girl ran at Keyonna, knocking her backward into a table and knocking it over. Quandra tried to get up, but I kicked her in the mouth as blood poured out almost immediately. I got on top of her and punched her in the face repeatedly.

She held her arms up to block me. "Lyric, stop! Stop!"

She yelled as I kept punching. The workers came from behind the counter, trying to pull me off of her as Keyonna picked up a knife and came at them. They ran back behind the counter as I continued punching Quandra while she screamed for me to stop. Blood from her mouth and her nose spread out in every direction as I got up, dragging her by the hair out of the restaurant. The customers pulled out their cell phones and recorded me as I pulled her out kicking and screaming.

"Bitch!"

I yelled out as I punched and kicked her a few more times until she was too beat up to protect herself. All of the rage that was buried inside of me from that day came out, and it was relentless. Keyonna got out the restaurant, grabbing me by the arm,

"Come on, we gotta go! They call the police!"

She ran to get in her car and pulled off. I walked back to the restaurant. One of Quandra's girls bled profusely from a stab wound as the workers gathered around her, doing their best to stop the bleeding. Her other friend was completely knocked out, laying across the floor. I grabbed Quandra's purse and pulled out all the money she had. *She owed it to me*, I said to myself as the workers yelled at me,

"Get the fuck out of here! We called the police!"

"Fuck you and the Muthafuckin' police!"

Quandra laid on the sidewalk outside the restaurant, bloodied and slowly regaining her strength. I punched her in the face one last time as the sirens buzzed in the distance. I knew they would be here any second as I drove out the parking lot. She only had a couple hundred dollars in her purse, but I didn't care. It wasn't even about the money. I had a taste of revenge, and it was sweet to the touch. It only made me want to go after Big Tuck even more. I knew if Nas saw what I did, he would stand and poke his chest out like a proud father.

Keyonna called me as I sped away from the restaurant. "Damn, bitch! At least warn me if you about to go fuck somebody up! I didn't know what the fuck was up at first!"

"My bad. That was some shit from a while ago. She must have thought I left the city again or some shit."

"I fucked that bitch up. She tried to stab me and shit, but I ended up putting that shit through her stomach."

"I saw it."

"Shit. You don't get to be Tuck's main bitch if you ain't willing to cut a muthafucka. I've done that shit before so it ain't nothing to do it again."

"Shit, I hear you."

"Well, meet me at the park. I'm almost there."

"Aight."

When we got to the park, she told me that Tuck was going to be free tomorrow, and he just wanted to fuck. She said she sent him pictures of me while she waited in the car and he knew me. *Suzy Rock?* he stated in the text. It sent an alarm to me because I didn't find out if he knew about my relationship with Junie. If he did, then he would know who I was, and everything me and Nas planned could go to shit real quick but I ignored it. This plan was set in stone, and nothing was going to change it. I had just tasted revenge, and I was too close to feeling it again to turn back.

Chapter 19

Big Tuck never fucked with new girls inside his crib. That's what he told Keyonna when she asked me to meet her at the hotel downtown. It was one of the high-priced suites at the Omni. I sat in the car with Nas a few blocks from the hotel. Loc and Man-Man sat in the front seats with loaded pistols ready for anything.

"How long you need before we come in there?"

"Umm… maybe like 15 minutes."

He looked at me with a side-eye. "That's a long ass time."

"I gotta' get him comfortable. Listen, nigga, just let me do this shit."

He huffed as spoke to Man-Man. "See, my nigga, you need a bitch like this. Somebody who ain't scared to talk to you any fuckin' way, even knowing you got bodies on you. That shit is sexy."

Man-Man didn't respond as he looked at me in the rearview mirror, then quickly turned back to observe the area we were parked in.

Keyonna texted me: *Bitch, where you at?*

I texted back: *I'm like five minutes away.*

Keyonna replied: *Aight, hurry up. You don't want to make that big muthafucka mad for waiting.*

I looked at Nas. "Baby, I gotta go."

"Aight." As I moved to get out the car, he grabbed me by my arm and pulled me back in, kissing me on the lips. "No fuckin."

I rolled my eyes and walked to my car that was parked just in front of theirs. When I pulled up, Keyonna was standing by the door anxiously waiting for me. Before I knew it, we were making our way up to the top floor.

"Now look," she said as she started prepping me for what was to come, "don't go in there doing anything different than what you did with me. I don't know if you're nervous or not but if you are, just be cool. Just suck his dick good and let him fuck you however he wants. And then," she smiled at me as the elevator beeped, passing each floor, "fuck the shit out of me. He likes to watch that shit."

The last beep sounded as we got off the elevator. Three men stood in the hallway with automatic rifles waiting for us. I recognized one of the guys immediately. He was the one that came up to my car when Junie went by one of Big Tuck's houses the night he got shot. He looked exactly the same besides a scar that was on the left side of his face.

He smiled at me, saying the same thing he said that night, "You Suzie Rock, ain't you?" a twisted smile plastered across his face. I ignored him and kept walking as he smacked my ass. I turned back towards him, but Keyonna grabbed my hand and pulled me back.

"Girl, just let it go."

He put his hands up the same way he did that night as if to say, "I don't want any trouble." He blew me a kiss as I turned and began walking down the hallway, arm in arm with Keyonna.

"Girl, you can't buck up at these niggas. These are Big Tuck's top dudes. Like, if they wanna fuck, then guess what? You fuck them. Plain and straightforward. Only one they can't fuck is me, but I was there where you was before. Shit, I fucked every dude you saw when we got off the elevator. That's just the type of shit that comes with the territory."

Her words went in one ear and out the other as we came to the door. She knocked twice, paused, and then knocked three times. A tall, slim man opened the door. He had bushy eyebrows and braids. His shirt hung from his body like it was too big for him to wear. In his hand, he gripped a 9-millimeter pistol. All black with a chrome handle.

"Whassup Fly?" Keyonna said as she pulled me past him and into the room. The size of it seemed like it would be able to fit four of five of the regular hotel rooms inside of this one. A luxury suite: two beds, a hot tub in the bathroom, big flat-screen TV mounted on the wall.

"Damn!"

"This?" she said, looking around the room. "This shit ain't nothing. This is just what he gets when he doesn't feel like spendin' a lot of money."

Just then, Big Tuck came out of the closet. He was shirtless, exposing his protruding stomach with no shame. His head was bald, and his beard grew out long and thick from his face. His skin was dark as the night sky above us.

"This that bitch you was talkin' bout, huh?" he said, walking over to the bed.

"Yeah, this her."

"Well shit, the fuck y'all standing there for? I got shit to do."

Keyonna set her purse down and started seductively pulling her clothes off. He turned to look at me, waiting for me to do the same thing. I walked over to the couch and put my purse down, pulling out my cell phone. I heard a bullet loading into the chamber of a gun, causing me to turn around to see the barrel aimed directly at me.

"Nah, bitch, ain't no fuckin' phones allowed in this muthafucka."

Keyonna's eyes widened as she rushed to me, explaining to Big Tuck on the way.

"Oh, she didn't know, Tuck. I'm sorry."

She looked at me and whispered sternly, "Girl, put that phone up! He doesn't want that shit up here."

"Nah!"

He yelled, the gun still aimed at me, "Bring that shit over here!"

I paused, looking back and forth between Keyonna and Big Tuck. Keyonna shook her head as if to say she couldn't help me,

"Did I fuckin' stutter? Bring that shit the fuck over here, bitch!"

I walked over to him as he snatched the phone from my hand,

"What's the passcode?"

"Why?"

He got up out the bed as quick as a man his size could.

"You fuckin' questioning me?! Bitch, I'ma ask you one more time," he said, reaching for the silencer that was on his nightstand,

"What is the fucking passcode."

"Lyric, just tell him the passcode."

"2-8-7-6."

He entered the code, scrolling through parts of my phone. He peered at me occasionally as his dark, ominous eyes went back and forth across my screen. I deleted every text, picture, and number that had anything to do with Nas before I came into the hotel. I knew that if he just so happened to ask for my phone that there was a possibility that he would go through it. Just like I told Nas, this was chess, not checkers. He took my phone and threw it against the wall, breaking it into several tiny pieces that scattered across the floor. With the gun placed firmly against my temple, he whispered to me,

"If you ever in your Muthafuckin' life bring a fuckin' phone around me again, I will kill yo' ass dead before you can even fix yo' lips to explain why the fuck you had it in the first place. You are here to fuck and suck my dick and leave. That's it, bitch. Now strip the fuck down and get on yo' knees so I can get the fuck on with my night."

I closed my eyes and took slow, deep breaths to calm myself down as he walked away. He kept the pistol in his hand as I looked over at Keyonna. She was completely naked, waiting for me to undress. As I started, she went over to him and rubbed on his dick until it got hard. Moments later, I heard her slobbering and sucking on it. He put his thick hand on top of her head, pushing it all the way down on his dick. He put the gun on his nightstand and waved me over with his finger when I was completely undressed. I walked over to the bed.

"Eat her pussy," he said to me.

I maneuvered my way under her and put my tongue on her pussy, licking it as I heard her choke on his dick. She shook her ass as I licked her lips and across her clit. He pushed her head off of him and reached forward, grabbing me by my hair and yanking me to his dick. He put his hand on top of my head and pushed it down, the same way he did Keyonna.

"Key, fuck her."

He said as she got up and walked to her purse, pulling out the same dildo she used when she fucked me in the car. As his dick went in my mouth, I felt her push the dildo inside of me. He moaned, pushing my head down further as I looked up at him. His eyes shut every now and then from the pleasure. The pistol was just out of reach on the nightstand. I would have to move up a little further to get it. Nas said he was going to come in right at 16 minutes, but if I could do this myself, I was going to do it. This was going to be my revenge, and it was what I planned all along. I went down further on his dick, putting it all the way down my throat. The times I fucked Keyonna helped me to understand how to handle all of it at once without gagging. She kept fucking me from behind, smacking my ass while I spat on his dick and jacked him off.

"Fuck!"

He yelled out as I went faster. She put the dildo deeper inside of me, and I slid up a little more because of it. I looked towards the gun as it was still out of reach. He opened his eyes, noticing I stopped, but I put my mouth back on his dick, sucking it hard and stopping to lick the tip of it, then shoving it back down my throat. Keyonna fucked me harder, moving me up more. Finally, the gun was within reach. I took his dick out of my mouth and reached for it, grabbing it off the table as I kicked Keyonna away from me. She flew back off the bed, hitting her head on the dresser. She was knocked unconscious as I turned to Big Tuck. His dick was hard, pointing straight to the ceiling as he looked at me, seemingly trying to process what was going on. After a few seconds, he caught on.

"Bitch, are you fuckin' crazy? You will be dead before you walk out this room."

"You remember Junie?" I said, aiming the gun directly at him. He laughed to himself as he turned to place his feet on the ground,

"Who the fuck is Junie?"

"Muthafucka don't play dumb! You had him killed almost a year ago."

He put his hand on his forehead. "Bitch, do you know how many people I kill every year? How the fuck am I supposed to remember based on that?"

He stood up, but I squeezed the trigger on the silencer, sending one bullet flying past him into the mattress.

"Sit yo' fat ass back down, nigga or the next one is going through your head."

He put his hands up and sat back down on the bed.

"Look bitch, I don't know no fuckin' Junie, and if I killed him, it was for good reason. Shit. Anybody I kill is for good cause."

He reached towards the nightstand as I fired another bullet into the pillow right next to him.

"Bitch, I'm just getting a cigarette."

He pulled it out of the drawer and lit the end of it, inhaling and blowing the smoke out slowly.

"Look, if I did kill him, he deserved it. Tuck don't kill anybody that didn't deserve it."

"Fuck that shit—"

"Oh, wait," he said, cutting me off, "I remember Junie. Hell yeah, tall, pretty ass muthafucka with the dimples? Hell yeah. He was short on some money he owed me. I gave him ample time to pay me back but the nigga just... drug his feet. He tried to hoe me. You know."

He blew smoke out of his mouth. "I can't let a pussy ass nigga like that hoe Big Tuck. This my city and I guarantee, if you kill me, you'll—"

Pow! The cigarette fell from his hand as he slowly tumbled over onto the floor, making a small thud. I shot him right in his forehead as the blood poured from his dome, forming a small puddle around him. My top lip curled up as I stood in front of his dead body, naked and empowered. I felt like the chapter of my life with Junie could officially close as he laid there, blood pouring out his body with his eyes wide open. I hurried and got dressed, keeping the gun close to me as if Big Tuck was going to get up from his gunshot wound and pull out another pistol.

It was well past 15 minutes by the time I got to the door. As soon as I cracked it open, I was staring down the pipe of a double barrel shotgun. I dropped my pistol when the round was loaded into the barrel.

###

Made in the USA
Middletown, DE
26 January 2019